Old Masters

T0364974

THE GERMAN LIST

Thomas Bernhard
Old Masters
A Comedy

Illustrated by
Nicolas Mahler

Translated by
James Reidel

Seagull
BOOKS

LONDON NEW YORK CALCUTTA

 GOETHE-INSTITUT

This publication was supported by a grant
from the Goethe-Institut, India

Seagull Books, 2018

The work *Alte Meister. Komödie* by Thomas Bernhard was first published
in 1985 by Suhrkamp Verlag, Frankfurt.

The graphic novel *Alte Meister. Komödie* by Thomas Bernhard and
Nicolas Mahler was first published in 2011 by Suhrkamp Verlag, Berlin.

ISBN 978 0 8574 2 470 9

British Library Cataloguing-in-Publication Data
A catalogue record for this book is available from the British Library

Typeset by Seagull Books, Calcutta, India
Printed and bound by Hyam Enterprises, Calcutta, India

Thomas Bernhard
Old Masters
A Comedy

Having arranged to meet Reger in the Art History Museum at eleven thirty in the morning, I was already there since ten thirty,

so that I could observe him at first unnoticed from the most ideal angle possible.

Since he has his morning place in the so-called Bordone Gallery opposite Tintoretto's *White-Bearded Man*, I had to position myself in the so-called Sebastiano Gallery,

thus, did I, entirely against my taste, have to put up with Titian so as to observe Reger before the *White-Bearded Man* by Tintoretto.

Irrsigler, the museum guard, with whom Reger had already been acquainted for over thirty years, had been alerted by a hand sign from me

that I wished to observe Reger unnoticed,

Irrsigler, for as long as I have known him, has always been the same pale white even though he isn't sick, and Reger, for decades, has referred to him as one of the state's dead bodies,

who has served the Art History Museum for thirty-five years.

Irrsigler said his greatest wish, ever since he had been a little boy, was to join the Vienna Police.

He had never wanted to be anything else.

But the police had dismissed Irrsigler for *physical weakness.*

In fact, Irrsigler only wanted to join the police because the police officer profession seemed to him to resolve the clothes problem.

To slip lifelong into the same uniform and never have to pay for this lifelong uniform, because the state provided it, seemed an ideal thing to him,

and there was too, in regard to this ideal thing, no difference whether he were employed by the police or the Art History Museum, however, the police pay more, the Art History Museum less,

but serving in the Art History Museum doesn't even compare to police service, for he, Irrsigler, could not imagine a more responsible but also easier job than in the Art History Museum.

Police work is surely life-threatening on a daily basis, so said Irrsigler,

working in the Art History Museum isn't.

You shouldn't worry about the monotony of his profession, he loves this monotony.

13

Irrsigler was rather surprised when he saw me today, for I had certainly said to him yesterday

that it was impossible

that I would be in the Art History Museum at the same time two days in a row.

And now we are both, Reger and me, in the Art History Museum,

in which we had been only yesterday.

Reger had expressly said to me yesterday,

Come here tomorrow.

I still hear the way Reger said that.

But Irrsigler had naturally heard nothing of this

and knew nothing about it

and naturally wondered

why Reger and I are in the museum again today.

Had Reger not said to me yesterday,

Come here
tomorrow,

I would not have gone to the Art History Museum
today,

this in contrast to Reger, who in fact goes to the Art History Museum every other day

and this for decades,

whereas I don't go to the Art History Museum every other day but, rather, only when I am in the mood.

I saw and observed Reger and heard at the same time what he said to me the day before.

The Art History Museum doesn't even have a Goya, not even an El Greco.

21

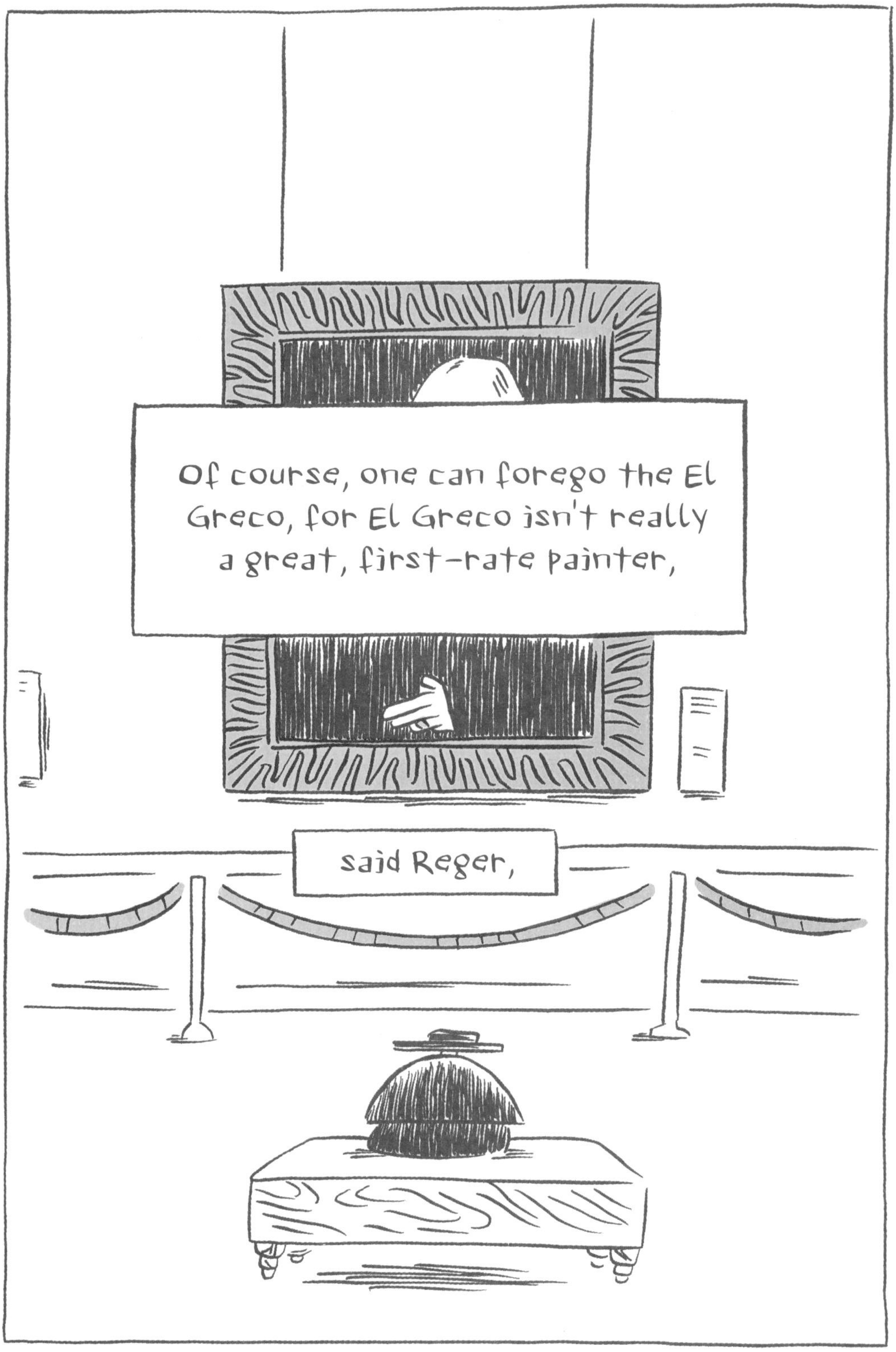
Of course, one can forego the El Greco, for El Greco isn't really a great, first-rate painter,
said Reger,

but for a museum such as
the Art History Museum
not to have a Goya is
categorically fatal.

Reger loves fog and gloom, he shuns the light,

which is also why he is inside the Art History Museum.

I hate going out for a walk, he says, it seems senseless to me.

I walk and walk during this going-out-for-a-walk and just think over and over

that I hate going out for a walk.

As you know, so said Reger, I surely don't go to the Bordone Gallery because of Bordone, not even because of Tintoretto.

26

I go for this bench in the Bordone Gallery

and because of the ideal influence of the light on my mental faculties, actually, to be precise, because of the ideal balance of temperature in the Bordone Gallery,

and because of Irrsigler,

who is only the ideal Irrsigler in the Bordone Gallery.

Actually, since childhood, I have had nothing but the museum, he said, I am by nature a museum-hater,

but I, for thirty years, actually come here for this very reason,

I have allowed myself this undoubtedly mentally related absurdity.

While others go to a taproom in the morning and drink three or four glasses of beer, I sit in here

and observe the Tintoretto.

Perhaps it's madness, as you must think, but I can do nothing else.

Where someone takes a bath at eleven in the morning, so as to get over his daily hurdles, I go to the Art History Museum.

Every person needs such a custom to survive, he said.

Only this custom has rescued me from the death of my wife.

Actually, I think that the Art History Museum is the only place of refuge, to vanish, which is dear to me, said Reger,

I must go to the old masters so that I can continue to exist, precisely to these so-called old masters,

whom I have hated a long time and for decades by now.

The Bordone Gallery is my thinking and my reading room. And if I have the desire for a sip of water, thus does Irrsigler bring me a glass,

never do I need to get up.

For years now, I have no longer read a book at home, while here in the Bordone Gallery I have already read hundreds of books,

but that doesn't mean that I have finished reading all these books, my way of reading is that of a highly talented page turner.

thus, of a man who turns dozens of pages, perhaps hundreds of pages,

before he even reads a single one.

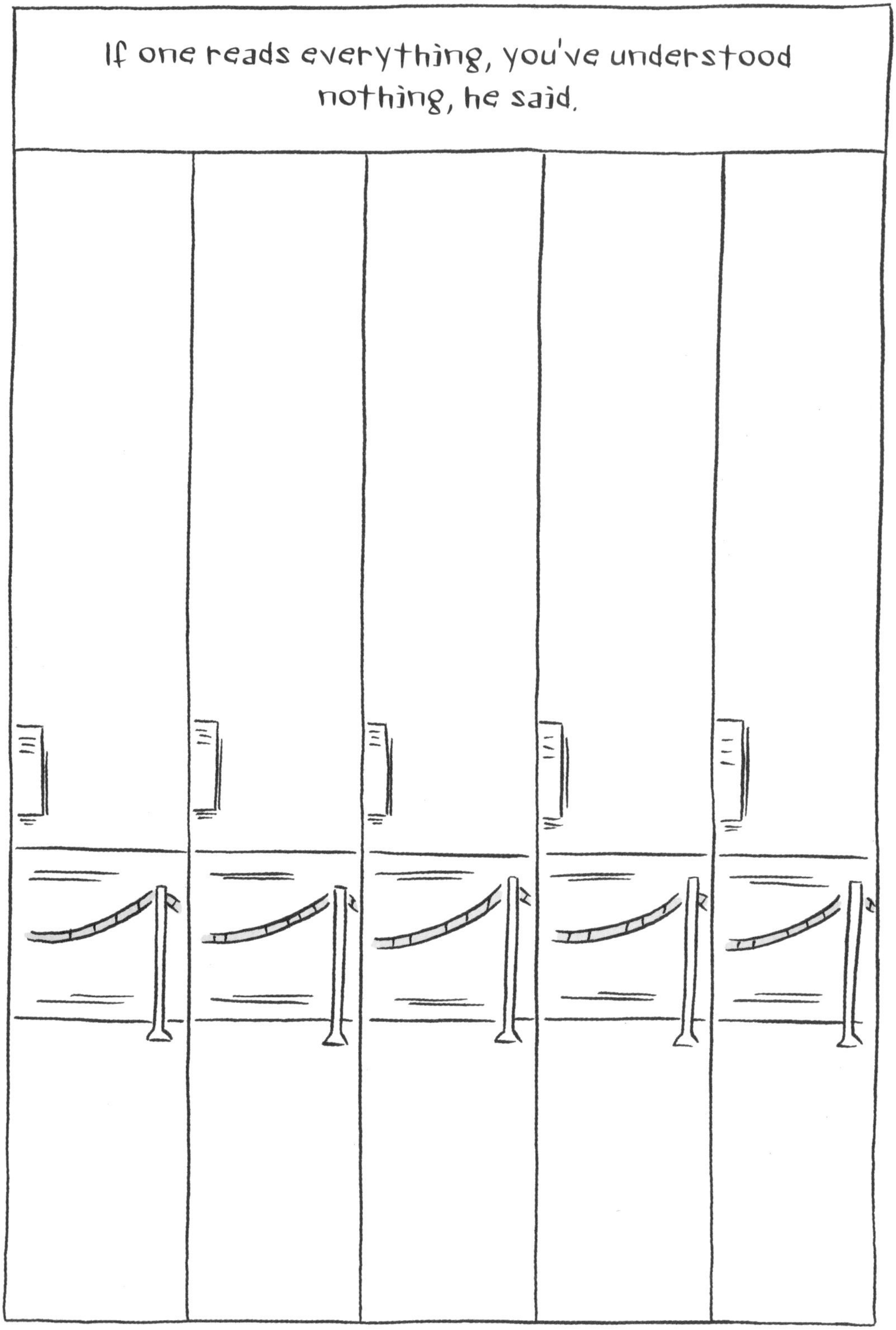
If one reads everything, you've understood nothing, he said.

We will understand a philosophical treatise better if we don't devour *the whole thing* in one go but, rather, by picking out some detail from which we can then arrive at the whole,

if we are lucky.

We surely derive the greatest pleasure from fragments,

while the whole, finished, perfect thing
ultimately leaves us appalled.

Only if we are lucky enough to turn some whole, finished thing, indeed, a perfect thing into fragments, do we maybe derive this great, indeed, the greatest pleasure in it.

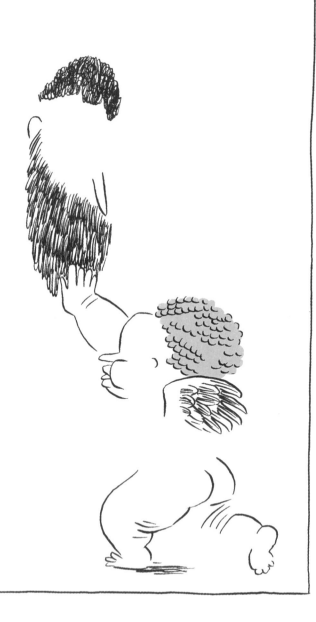

We will not survive the whole, the perfect thing.

We must go to Rome and see that St Peter's is a tasteless piece of work,

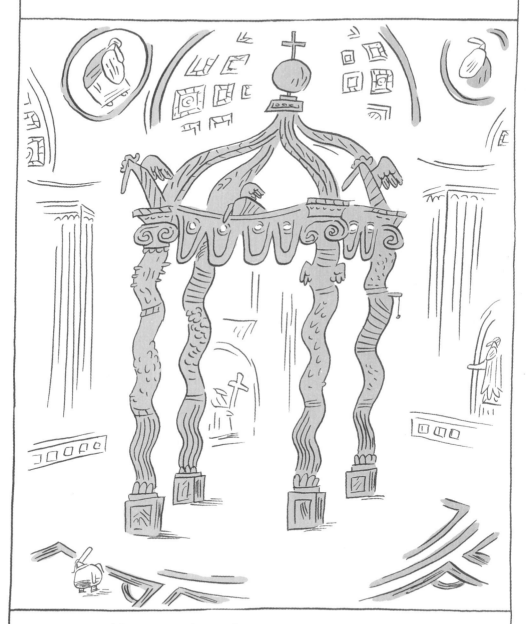

the Bernini altar, architectural mindlessness, he said.

We must see the Pope face to face and *see first hand* that he is, all in all, a helplessly grotesque man, the same as everybody else as well,

so that we can stand it.

There is no perfect painting and there is no perfect book and there is no perfect piece of music,

said Reger,

that is the truth.

None of these world-famous masterpieces, no matter who did them, is actually something whole and perfect.

This reassures me, he said.

In essence, this makes me happy.

Only when we unswervingly come to the realization that there isn't this whole or perfect thing do we have any possibility of survival.

And that has been the reason why I have gone to the Art History Museum for over thirty years and not the Natural History Museum across the street.

I heard Reger say yesterday, while I observed him now from the Sebastiano Gallery.

Not to mention that all of these so-called old masters have only painted but one detail of their paintings with any real brilliance,

not a single one of them has painted a hundred per cent brilliant painting, not one of these so-called old masters has ever executed this.

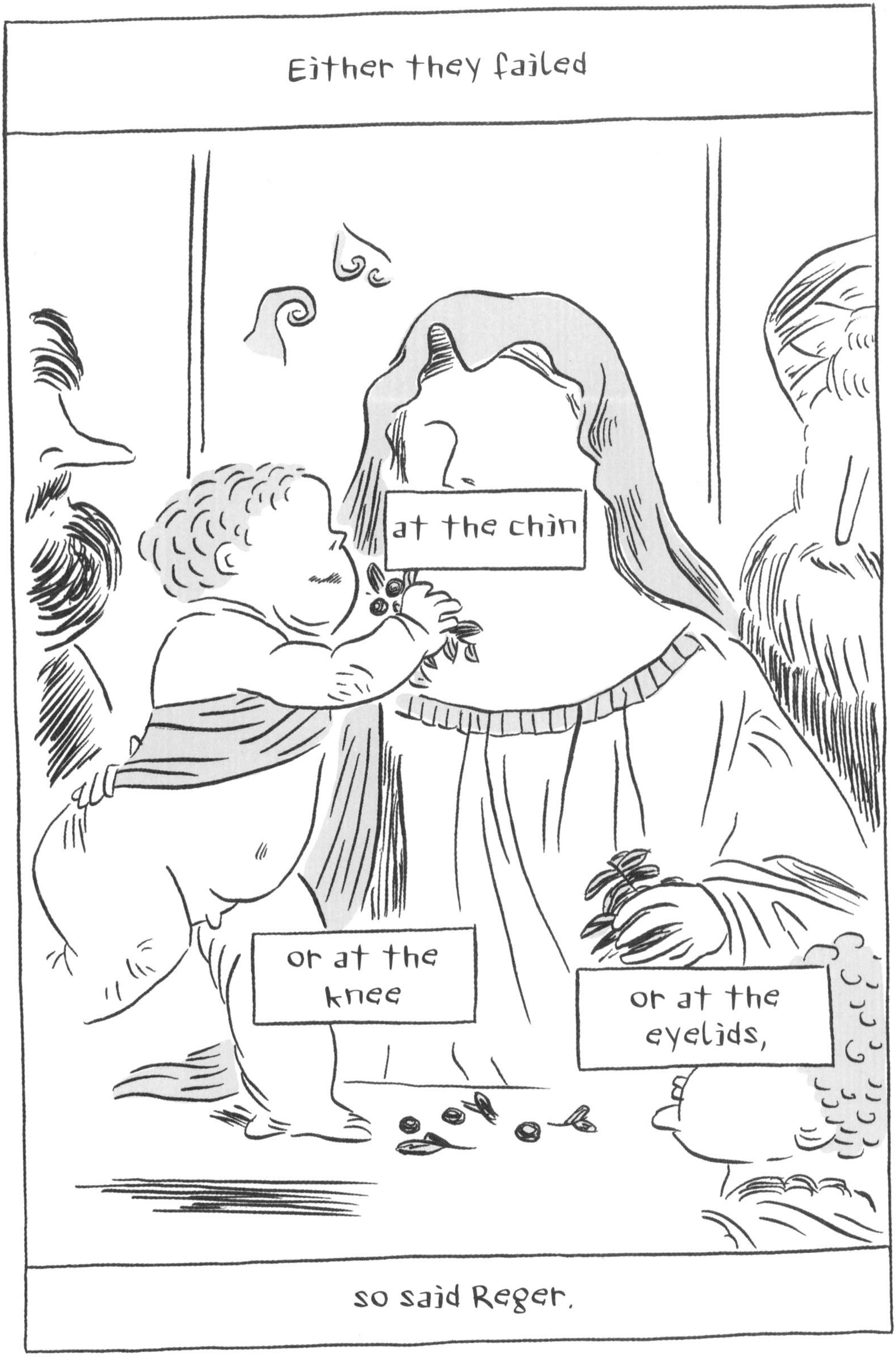
Either they failed
at the chin
or at the knee
or at the eyelids,
so said Reger.

Most failed at the hands, there is not a single painting in the Art History Museum in which one might see a brilliantly painted or even an exceptionally painted hand,

only these failed hands in such a tragi-comic way, so said Reger.

The artists, the so-called great artists, so said Reger, I think, are the most unscrupulous of all people,

they are as unscrupulous as politicians,

The so-called old masters are, before anything, if one considers their works of art side by side,

mendacity enthusiasts,

who have curried favour and sold themselves out to the tastes of the Catholic state.

In Europe they have only ever painted into the hands of a Catholic God and up to his face, he said,

a Catholic God and his Catholic gods.

The painters have not painted what they should have painted but, rather, what they have been told to or what delivered or brought them

money or fame.

These old masters are nothing more than the decorative accomplices and religious falsifiers of their European Catholic masters,

you see this in every dab of paint which these artists have blatantly squeezed on their canvases.

Look at the Velazquez,

nothing but state art,

the Lotto, the Giotto,

only state art,

like this terrible ur- and pre-Nazi Dürer, this atrocious Dürer,

this Nuremberg etcher.

The painters, all these old masters who most of the time disgust me like nothing else and have horrified me all along,

he said,

are no good, indeed, they always have a very bad character and for this reason too, essentially, they always display very bad taste.

The dreadful thing is that I find these old masters profoundly despicable and yet I am always studying them.

But they are repulsive, that is quite clear, he said yesterday.

The old masters can only withstand superficial analysis. If we put them under intense analysis, they gradually fade away and in the end dissolve, they crumble before us

and only leave a bland, indeed, a rather foul taste in our heads at most.

The largest and the most important work of art is as oppressive to us as an enormous chunk of vulgarity and lies in one's head

like some far too large chunk of meat in one's belly.

We are fascinated by a work of art and in the end it is only ridiculous.

There is also this technique, he said yesterday,

as I observed him now, a day later, from the side,

there is also this technique to make everything a cartoon.

We can survive a large, important painting only
if we turn it into a cartoon.

But most people are incapable of a cartoon, they regard everything in the end with their dreadful earnestness.

They have an audience with the Pope, he said, and take the Pope and the audience seriously

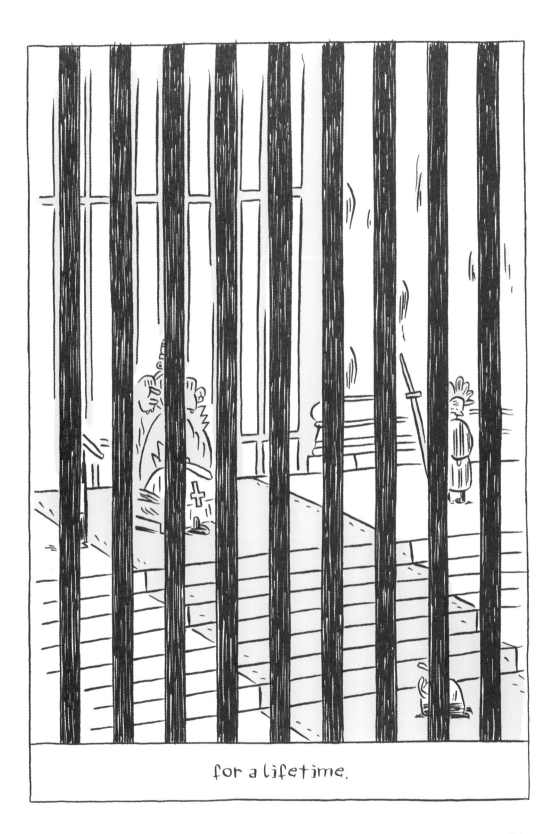

for a lifetime.

Nothing repels me as much as when I see people who admire,

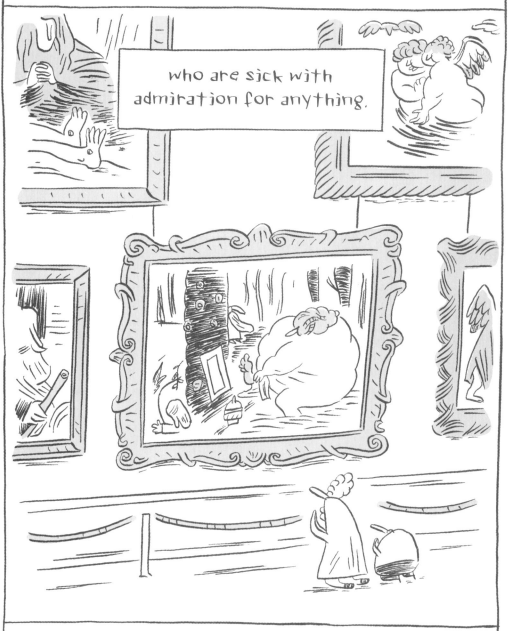

who are sick with admiration for anything.

Most people just go through life simple-minded, solely because they admire.

The condition of admiration is a condition of mental weakness, said Reger yesterday,

almost everyone exists in this condition of mental weakness,

In this condition of mental weakness, they all enter the Art History Museum too, he said.

The people slog weighed down in their admiration,

they haven't the courage to surrender their admiration to the cloakroom, like their coats.

There is nothing to admire, said Reger yesterday,

not

one thing,

nothing.

75

Velazquez, Rembrandt, Giorgione, Bach, Handel, Mozart, Goethe, he said, even Pascal, Voltaire,

such loud, inflated monstrosities.

That *Stifter*, he said yesterday, is as much a poor writer when given thorough commitment

as Bruckner is a poor, if not miserable composer when given an intensive hearing.

Stifter writes in a terrible style and whose grammaticality is beneath contempt at that.

Stifter is a kitsch master.

There is enough kitsch on any random page of Stifter to satisfy more than one generation of poetry-thirsty nuns and nurses.

Actually, Stifter has always made me think of *Heidegger*, of that ridiculous National Socialist, knickerbocker-wearing philistine.

Heidegger is the slipper- and night-cap philosopher of the Germans, nothing more.

I can't see Heidegger any other way, on that picnic bench outside his Black Forest cottage, next to his wife, who lorded over him totally for his entire life and knitted him every pair of stockings and crocheted every one of those caps.

I have seen a series of photographs, which I will show you, said Reger. In these photographs,
Heidegger gets out of bed,
Heidegger gets back into bed,
Heidegger sleeps,
he wakes up,
he puts on his underpants,
he pulls on his stockings,
he drinks some cider,
he walks out of his log house,
and looks into the horizon,

he takes his cap from his head,
he puts his cap on,
he holds his cap in his hands,
he reads,
he spoons his soup,
he cuts himself a slice of (home-baked) bread,
he opens a (self-written) book,
he closes a (self-written) book,
he bends, he stretches and so on, said Reger.
It's enough to make you puke.

I look at the time,

it was ten minutes before eleven thirty.

One reason why I was in the museum by ten thirty was to be punctual, for Reger requires nothing more than

punctuality.

Reger is the most punctual person I know. He has

never arrived late in his life, at least not intentionally,

as he says.

Unpunctuality is a disease which is fatal to the unpunctual,

so said Reger once.

Reger exited the Bordone Gallery after Irrsigler whispered something into his ear.

But since I had agreed with Reger

in this very
Bordone Gallery

to meet at eleven thirty

and Reger is the most punctual and reliable person

that I know,

Reger will return to the Bordone Gallery precisely at eleven thirty,

I thought,

89

and hardly had I thought this,

when Reger returned to the the Bordone Gallery.

At eleven thirty on the dot he glanced at the pocket watch, pulled from his coat pocket with lightning-like speed

as I, at the same time, entered the Bordone Gallery from the Sebastiano Gallery.

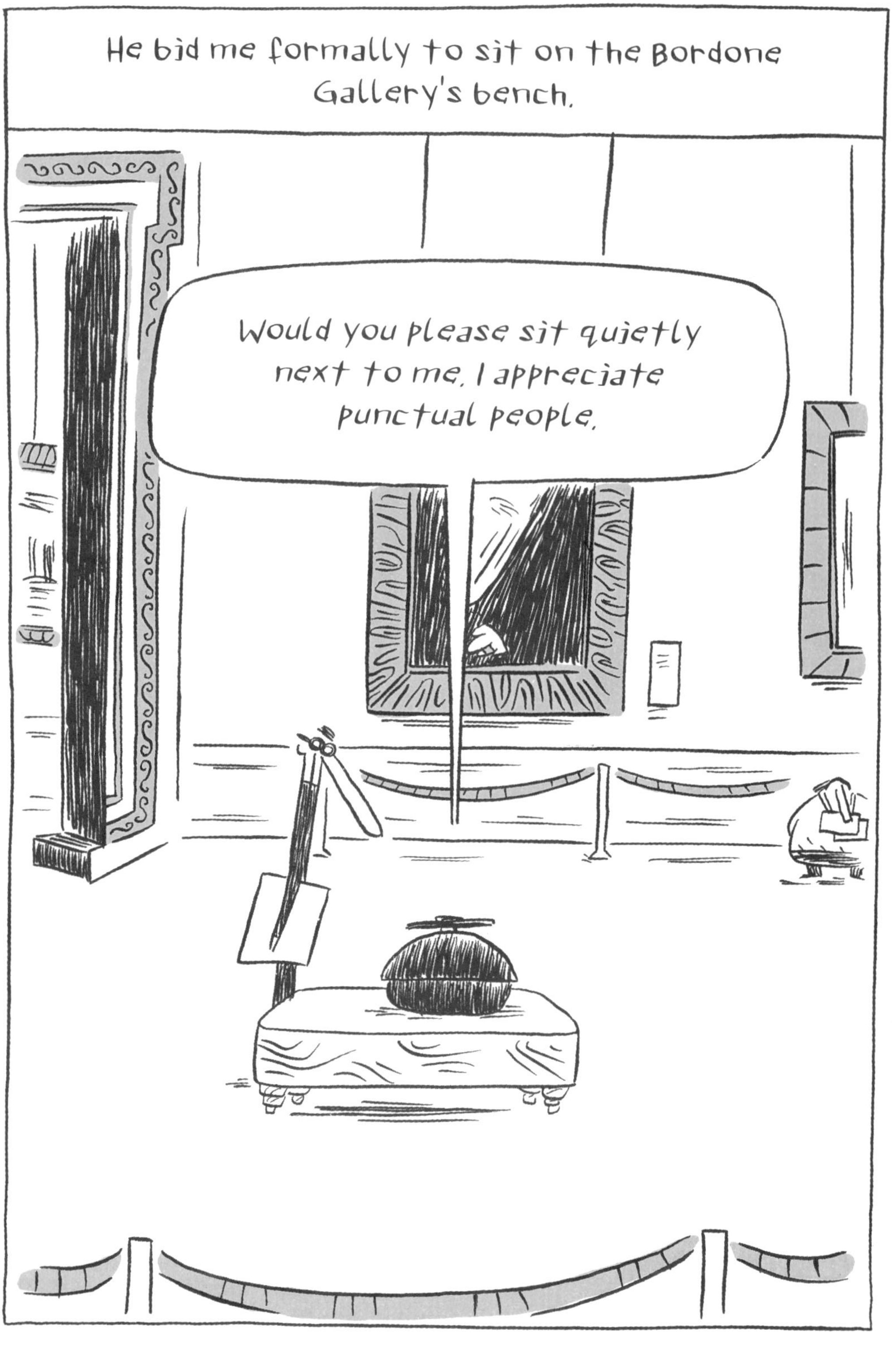
He bid me formally to sit on the Bordone Gallery's bench.
Would you please sit quietly next to me. I appreciate punctual people.

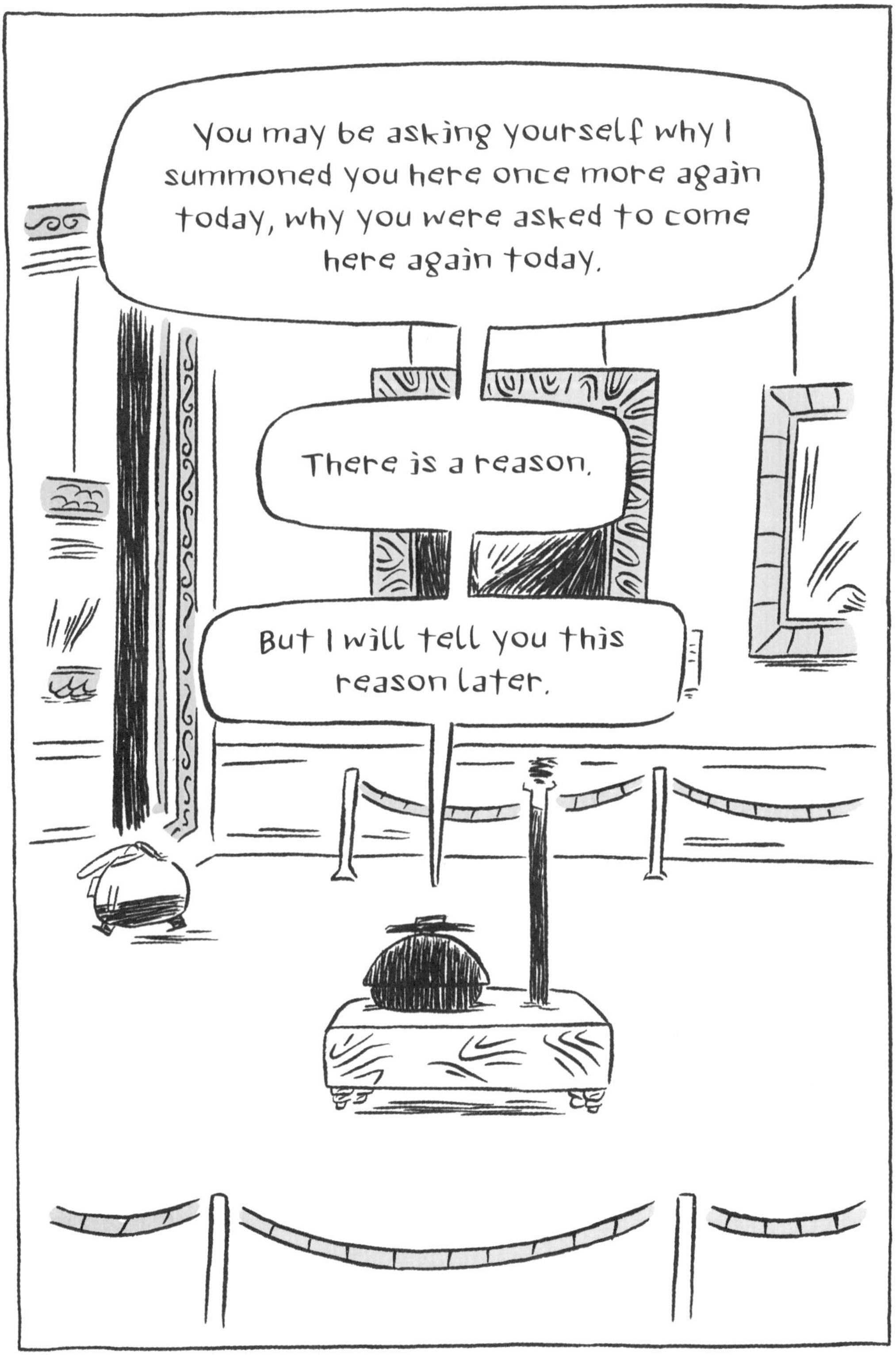
You may be asking yourself why I summoned you here once more again today, why you were asked to come here again today.
There is a reason.
But I will tell you this reason later.

I don't know how I should tell you this reason.

I don't know.

I have been thinking about it the whole time
and I don't know.

I have already been here for hours and thinking about it

and I don't know.

Irrsigler is my witness, said Reger, I have been sitting here for hours and thinking about it, how I should tell you, why I asked you to the Art History Museum today as well.

We commit a crime and are incapable of simply admitting to it without ceremony, said Reger.

I have already told Irrsigler, but I cannot tell you yet, he said,

it is really embarrassing.

Do you know where I met my wife? he said,

I met my wife in the Art History Museum,

And do you know where in the Art History Museum, he asked,

and, of course, I thought I knew where in the Art History Museum, and he said,

here in the Bordone Gallery, on this bench.

In this way he said this, as though he no longer really knew that he had already told

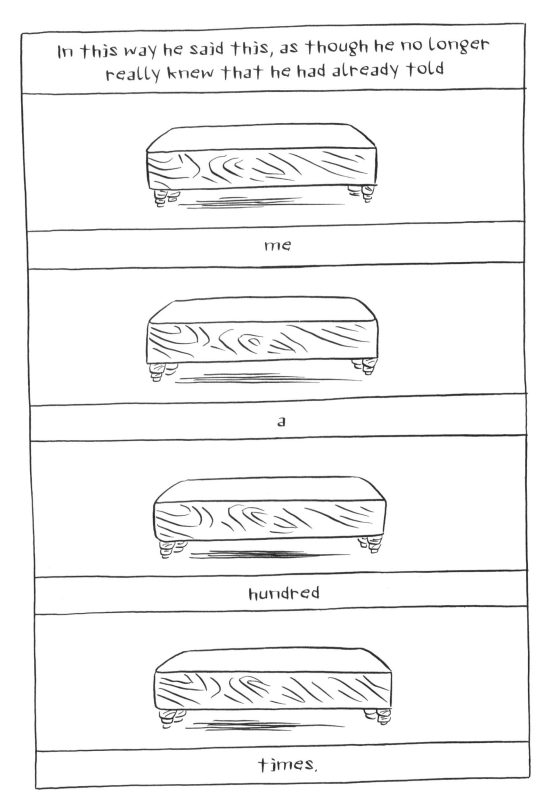

me

a

hundred

times.

It was a dull day, he said, I was desperate, and I sat here on the this bench and was pondering over a certain Schopenhauerian proposition,

I can't say anything more about which proposition, he said.

when suddenly this stubborn woman sat down on the bench beside me and remained sitting.

The woman sat there and stared at the *White-Bearded Man*, said Reger, and I believe she stared at the *White-Bearded Man* for an hour.

Do you like the *White-Bearded Man* by Tintoretto that much?

I had never heard such a no until this no.

Not long after, we were married.

We sit on this bench, mentally and even spiritually abandoned, said Reger, and are more or less this deformation of ourselves,

this hopelessness, meant Reger,

and then a woman sits down next to us and we marry her

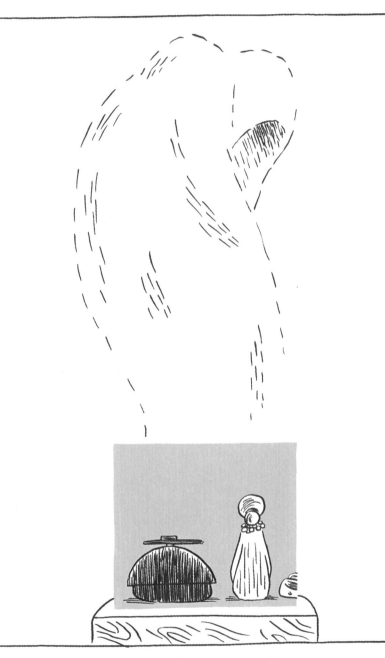

and are saved,

Millions of married couples have met on a bench, said Reger,

this fact is absolutely one of the most vulgar there is.

For nearly a half year after the death of my wife, I no longer went to the Art History Museum,

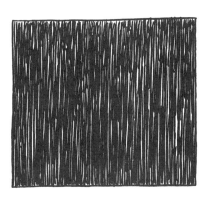

then after a half year, I came here once again,

but, naturally, at first not every other day as usual,

but rather no more than once per week.

For half a year I avoided all contact with people,

because I wanted get away from their dreadful questions,

people are always the least inhibited when making these inquiries about someone's death

and at every opportunity;

109

I wanted to escape them, so that I only had Irrsigler.

Irrsigler was, because he usually never asked me anything, the only person possible, said Reger.

111

Essentially, Reger said once, I died too the moment my wife died.

The truth is that I exist as a corpse, like a corpse which is still alive.

We no longer want to live on any longer when we have lost the people who are closest to us, but we must continue to live on,

we don't kill ourselves because we are too cowardly to do so.

The mere fact that I had to do so much running around in connection with the funeral left me no time to kill myself.

When we don't kill ourselves *immediately*, we will never kill ourselves, that's the appalling thing, he said.

Naturally, we get used to a person for decades and love them for decades and chain ourselves to them and when we lose them, it is true,

it's as if we lost everything.

I have always believed

that it is music that means everything to me,

sometimes, too, that it is philosophy,

the high and the highest and the highest of all writing,

if anything, art is quite simple, but all of this, all of this art, however,

is nothing compared to this one, single beloved person.

All our lives we abandon ourselves to these great men, these spirits of the ages and these so-called old masters, so said Reger, and we are fatally disappointed by them, for they never fulfil their end

at this crucial moment.

And you realize, these are not great minds and these are not old masters, whom you held in esteem for decades of your life, but that it has been

this single one person, whom you have loved like no other.

We believe we can manage without people,

yes, we even believe that we can manage
without a single person

and we imagine we can as well, that we have just one opportunity when we are alone with ourselves,

but that is a pipe dream.

We hate people and yet we want to be together with them,

since we are only with people and among them have a chance to survive and not go crazy.

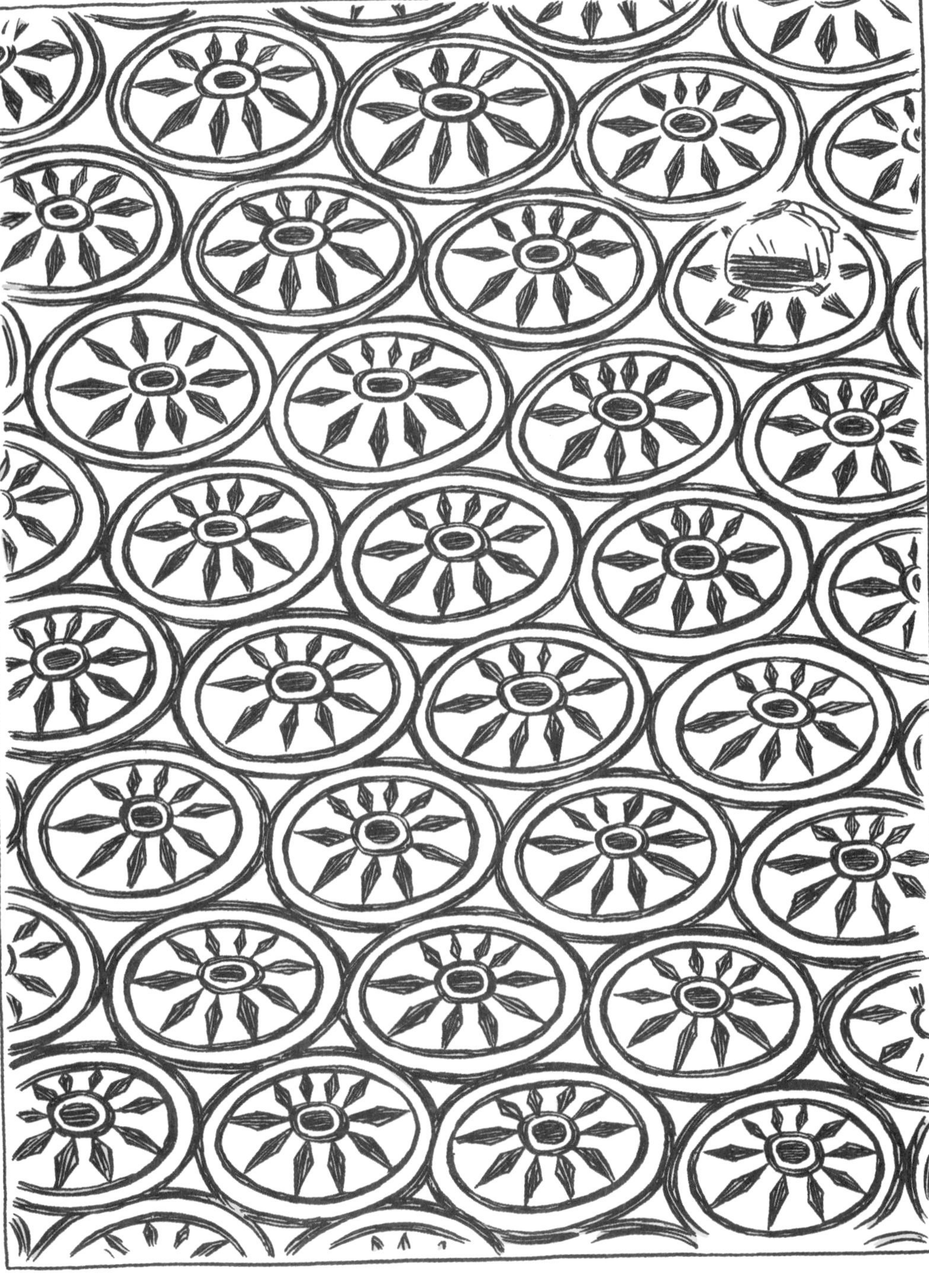

We could have accepted so many great minds and so many old masters as companions,

but they are not a replacement for people, so said Reger,

in the end we are, by all these so-called great minds and these so-called old masters,

left alone

and we see that we will be mocked by these great minds and old masters in the most vulgar ways,

Everything here in the Art History Museum, said Reger now, means an end for us, namely,

at this decisive point of our existence,

nothing more.

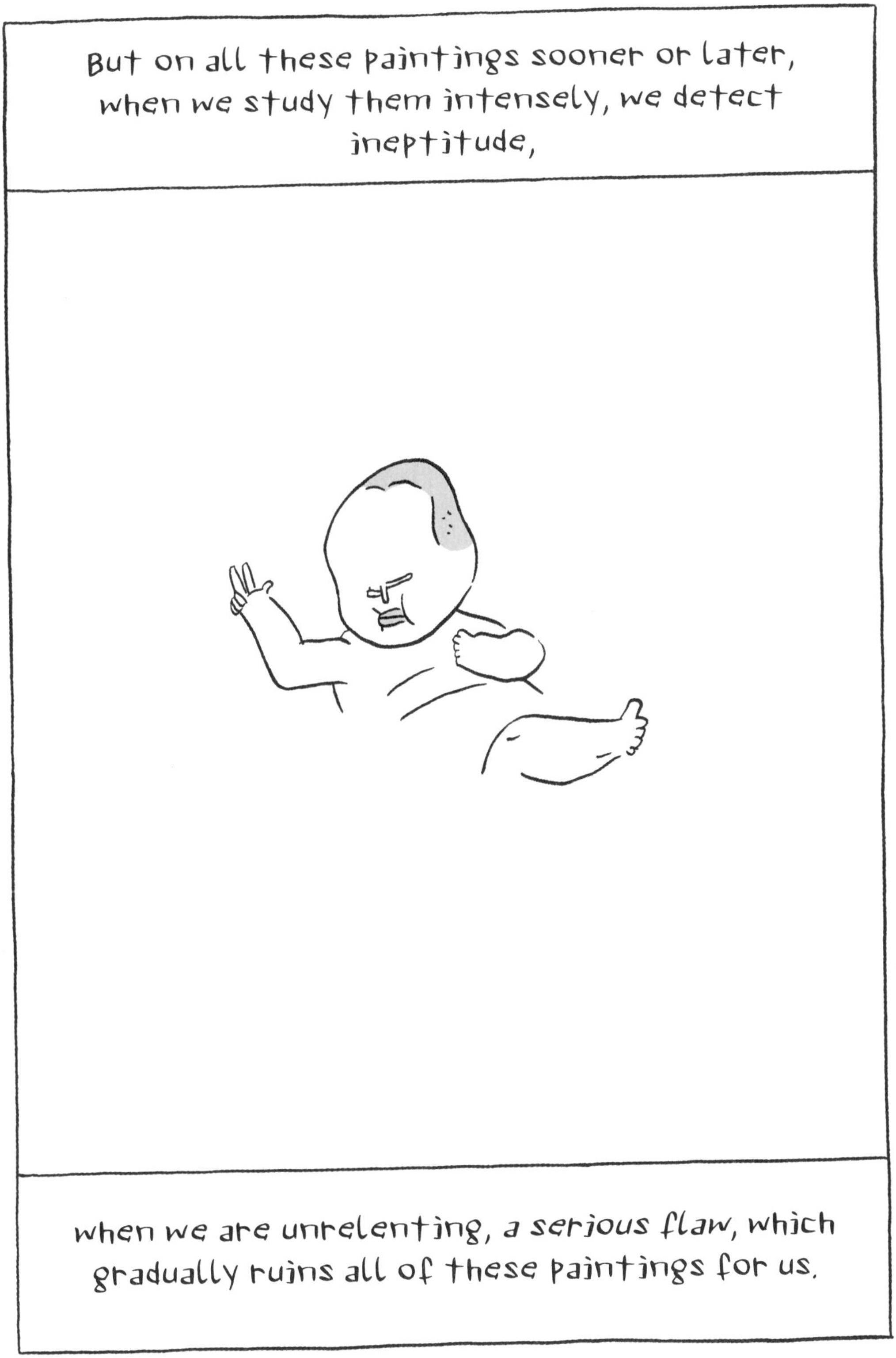

But on all these paintings sooner or later, when we study them intensely, we detect ineptitude,

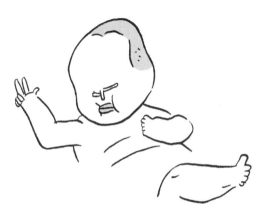

when we are unrelenting, a serious flaw, which gradually ruins all of these paintings for us.

Too, art is by and large nothing other than an art of survival,

all in all it is for ever this attempt made to cope with the world and all its repulsiveness and done so in a reasonably touching way.

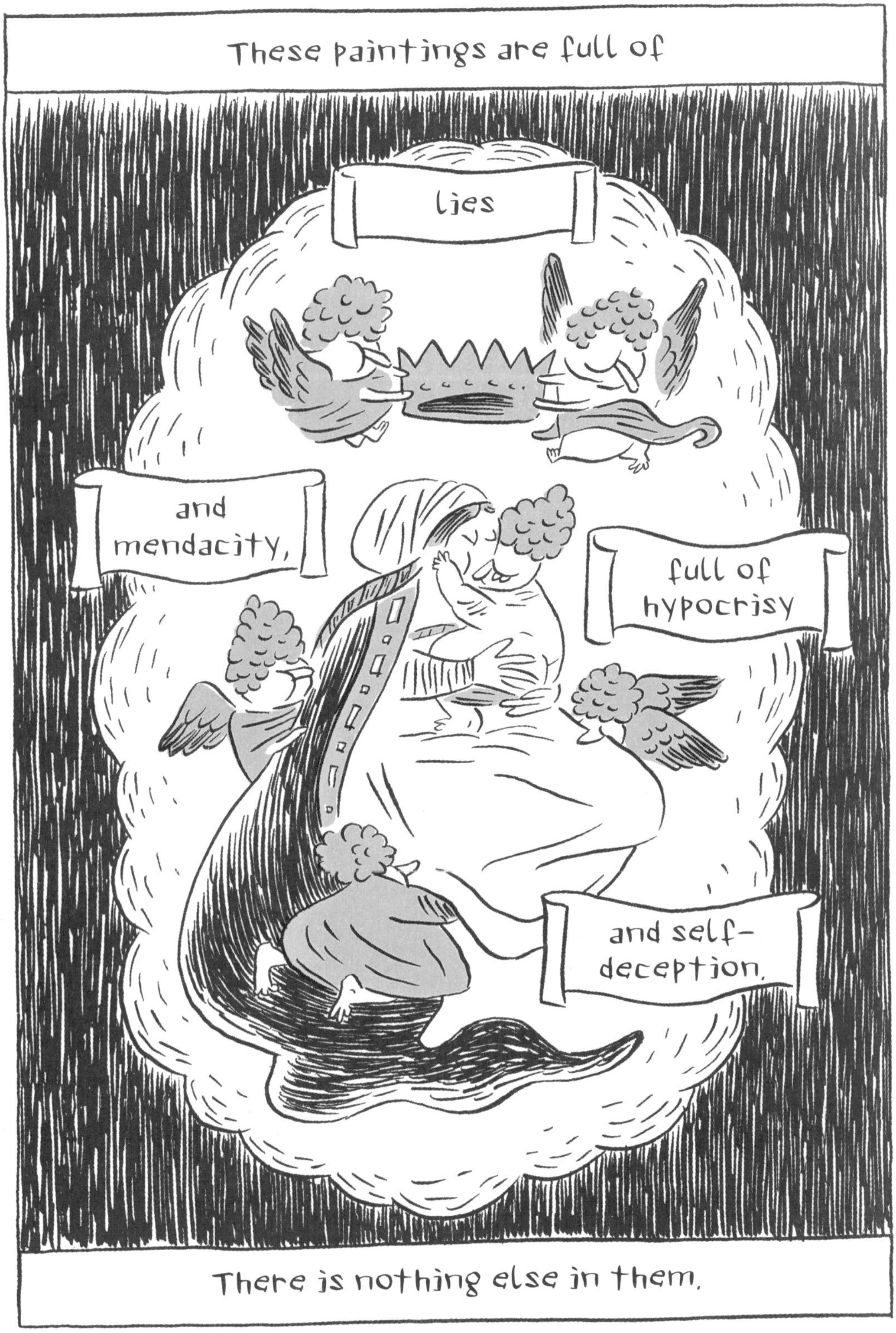
These paintings are full of
lies
and mendacity,
full of hypocrisy
and self-deception.
There is nothing else in them.

Furthermore, all these paintings are an expression of humankind's utter helplessness to cope with themselves and with that which surrounds them for a lifetime.

All of these paintings, those on the one hand which are humiliating to a thinking person, and those on the other which are disturbing to that same thinking person, express this and a touching helplessness to death, so said Reger:

The White-Bearded Man, for over thirty years, has withstood my mind and my feelings, so said Reger,

for this reason he is the most valuable one exhibited here in the Art History Museum,

Art is the highest thing and the most despicable thing at the same time, he said.

But we must persuade ourselves there is this high and highest art, he said, otherwise we fall into despair.

Even when we know that all art ends up in ineptitude and ludicrousness and in the rubbish of history,

like everything else too.

No matter what we think and no matter what we discuss and believe, we are competent and yet are not,

this is the comedy,

and when we ask, how does it go on,

there is the tragedy.

Irrsigler appeared and brought the *London Times*, which Reger had requested of him,

he just needed to walk across the street, where there is a news-stand outside the Art History Museum.

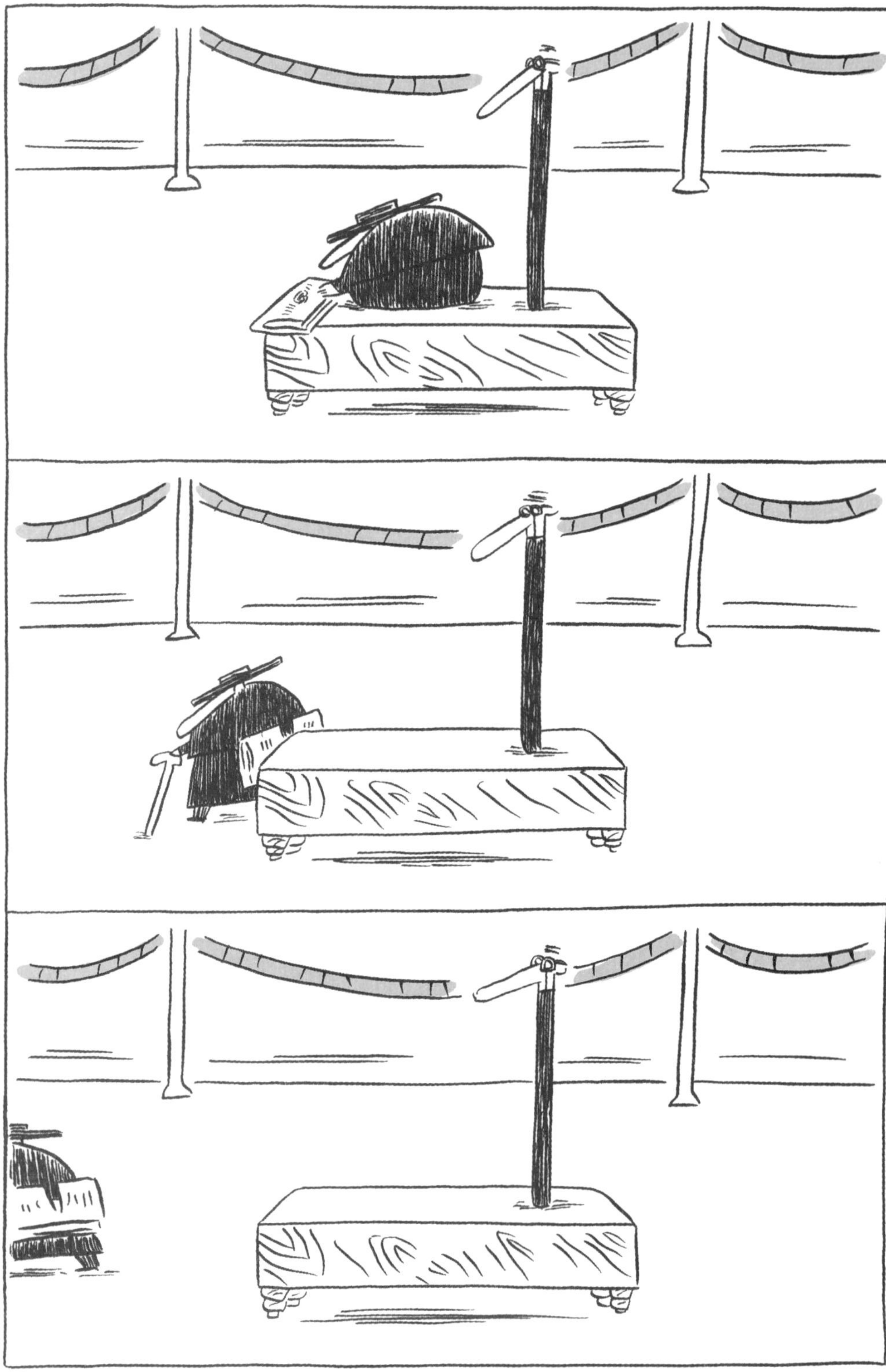

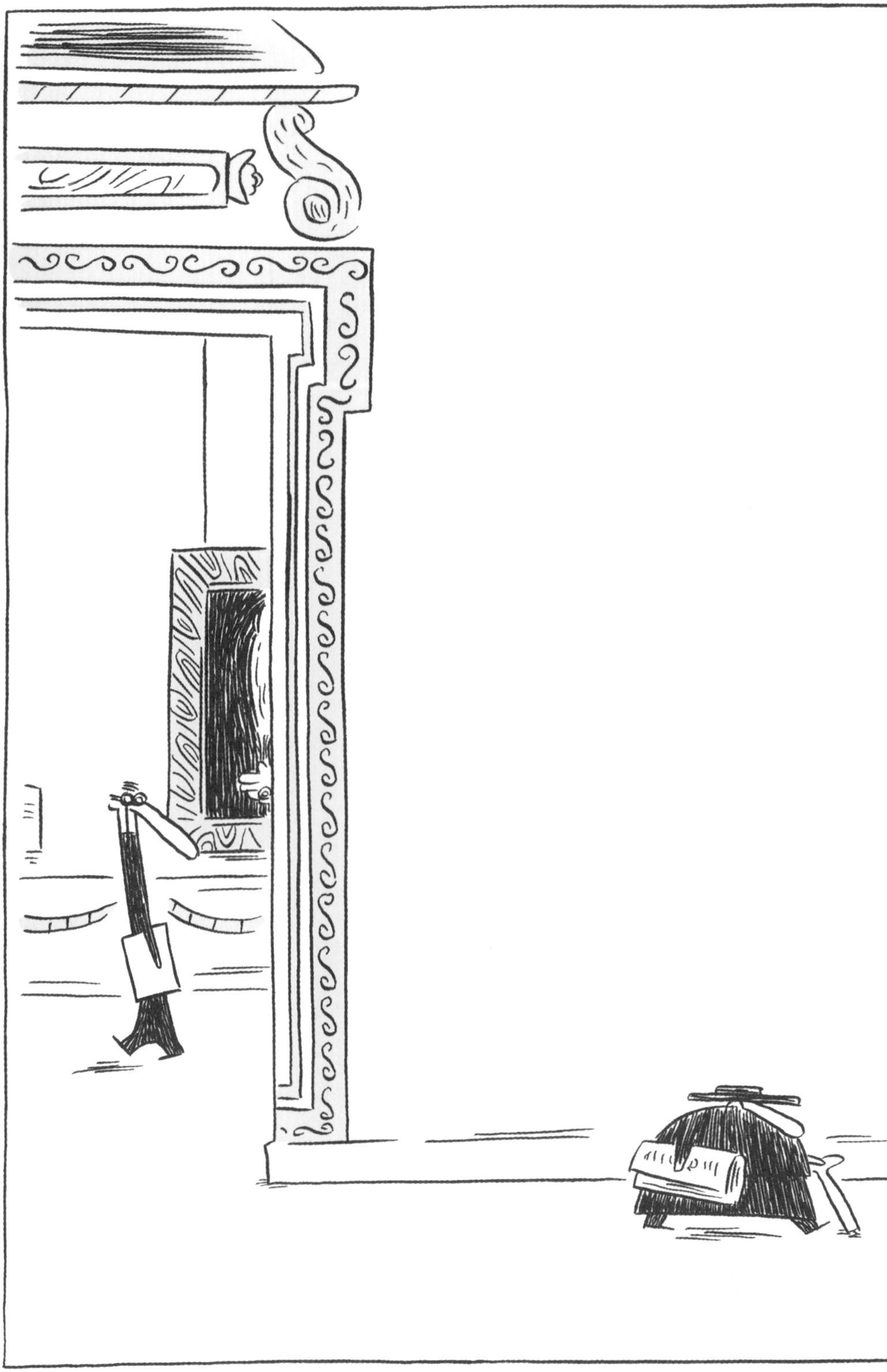

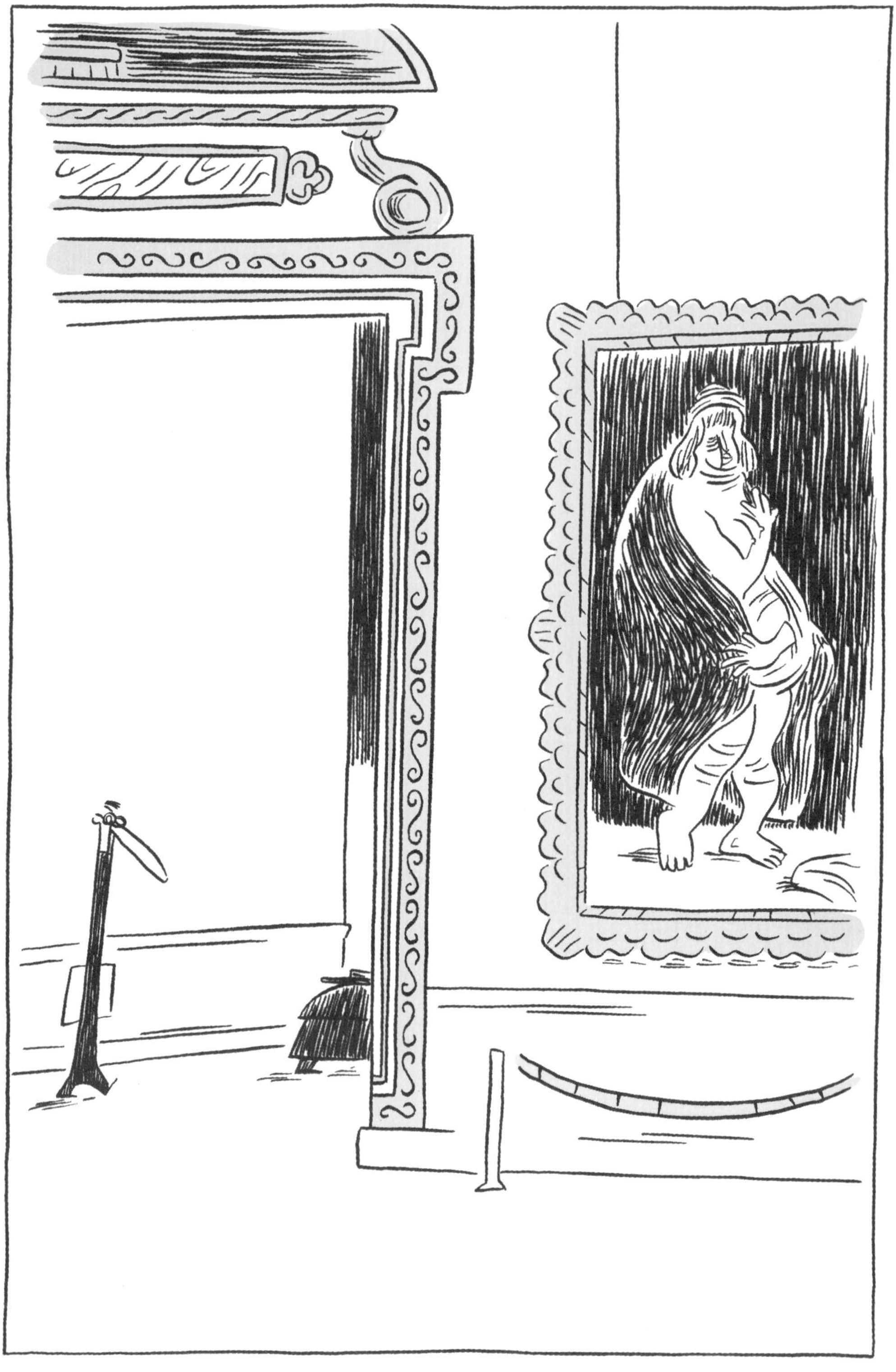

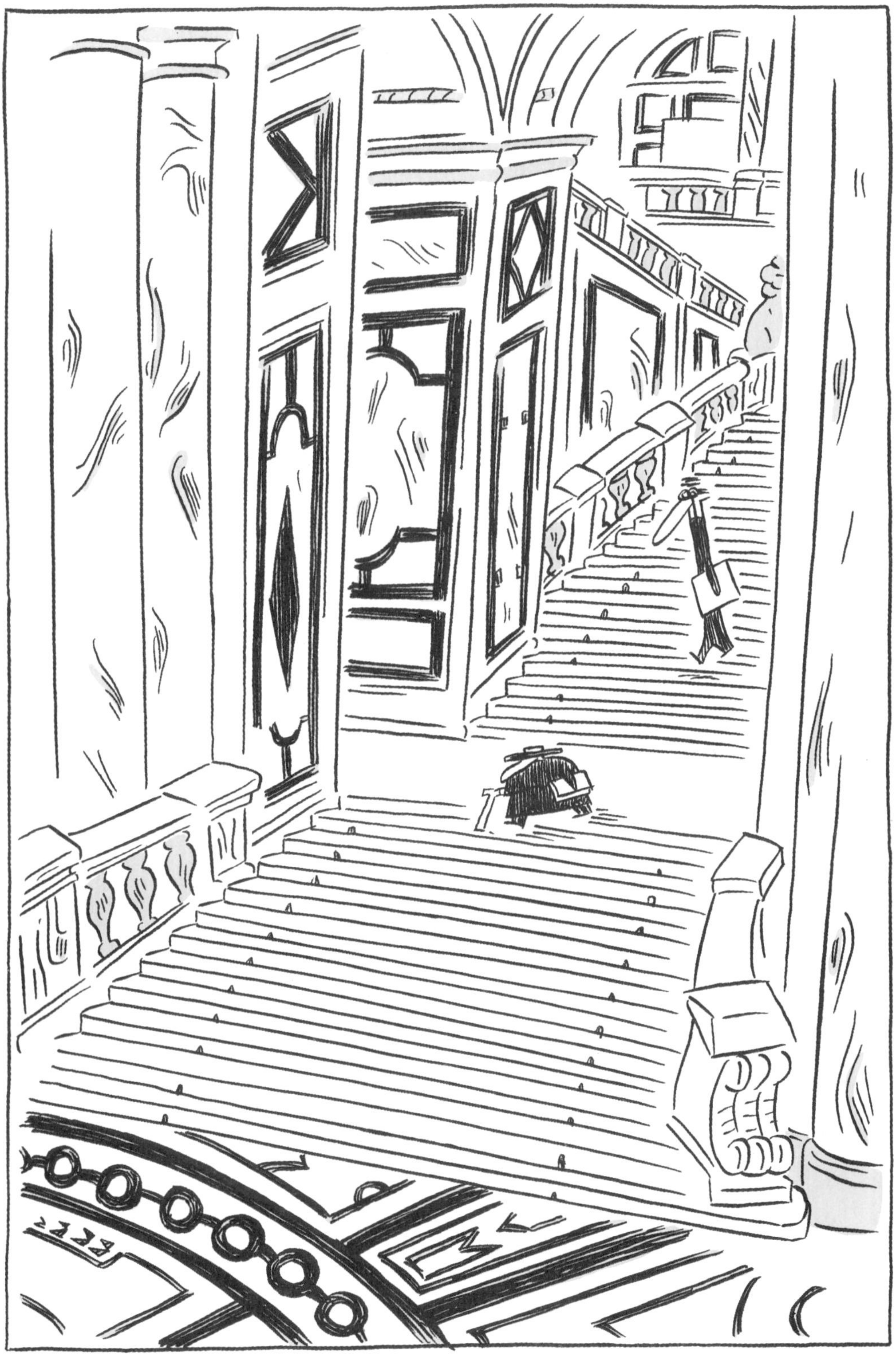

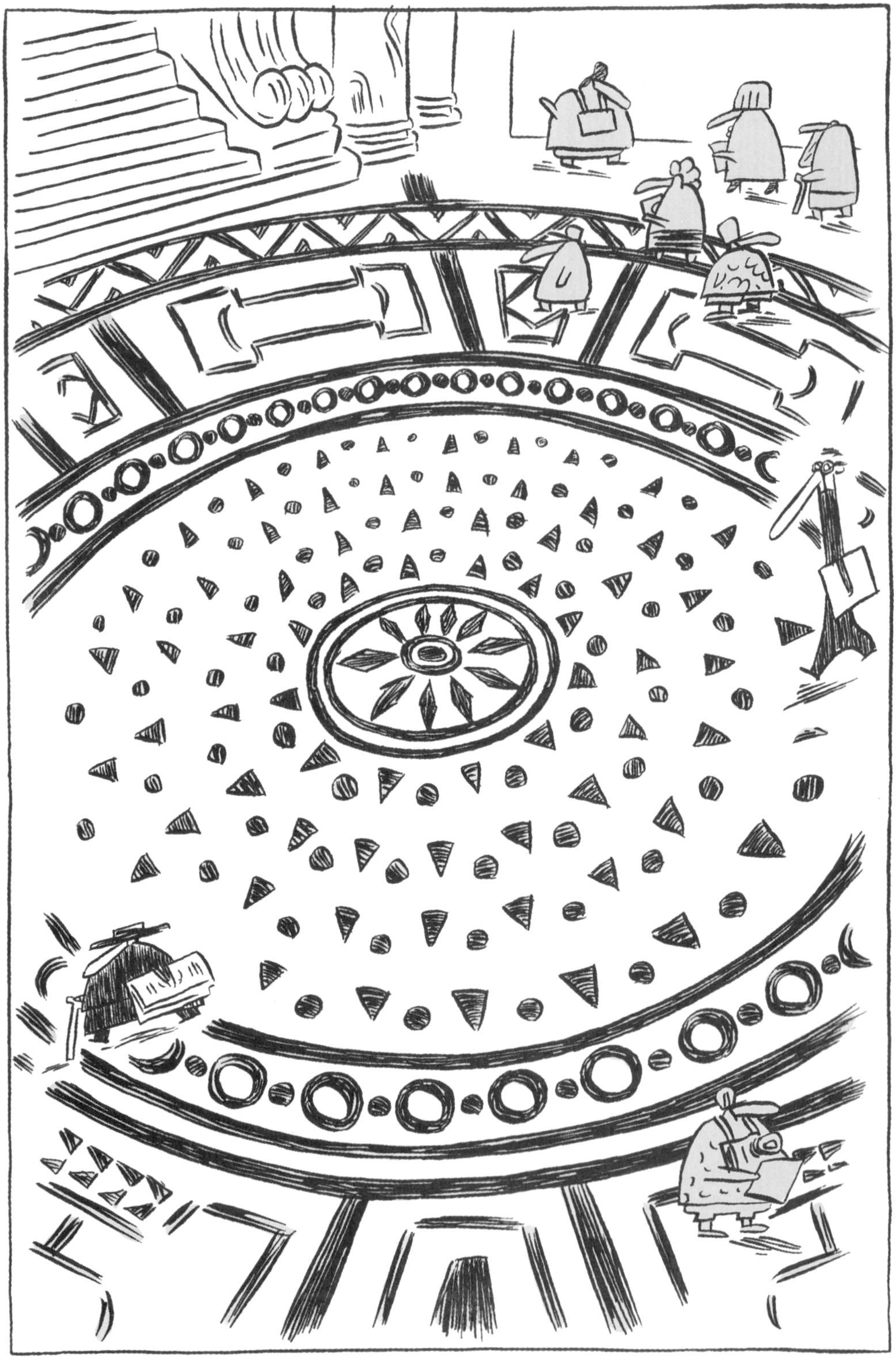

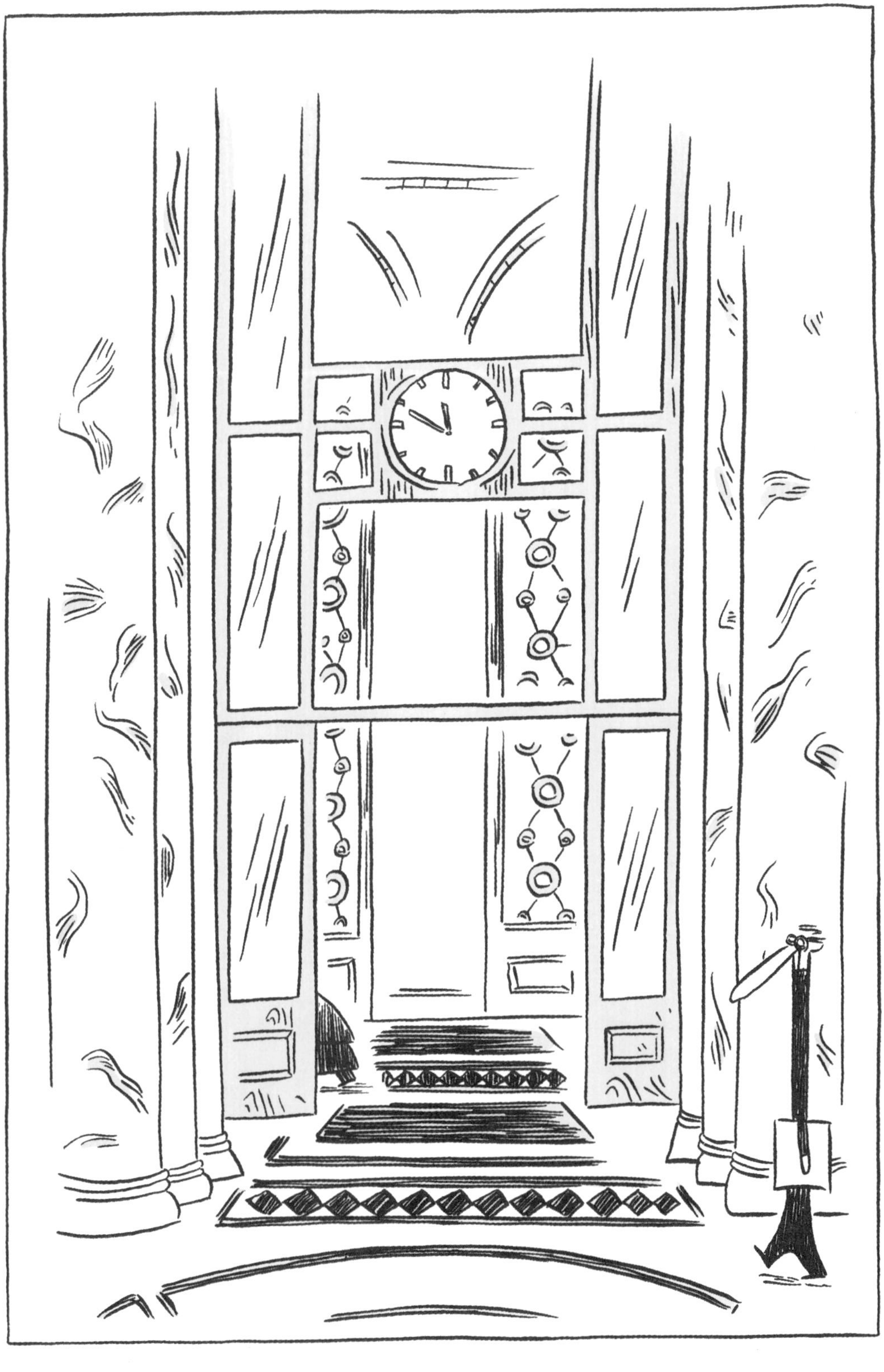

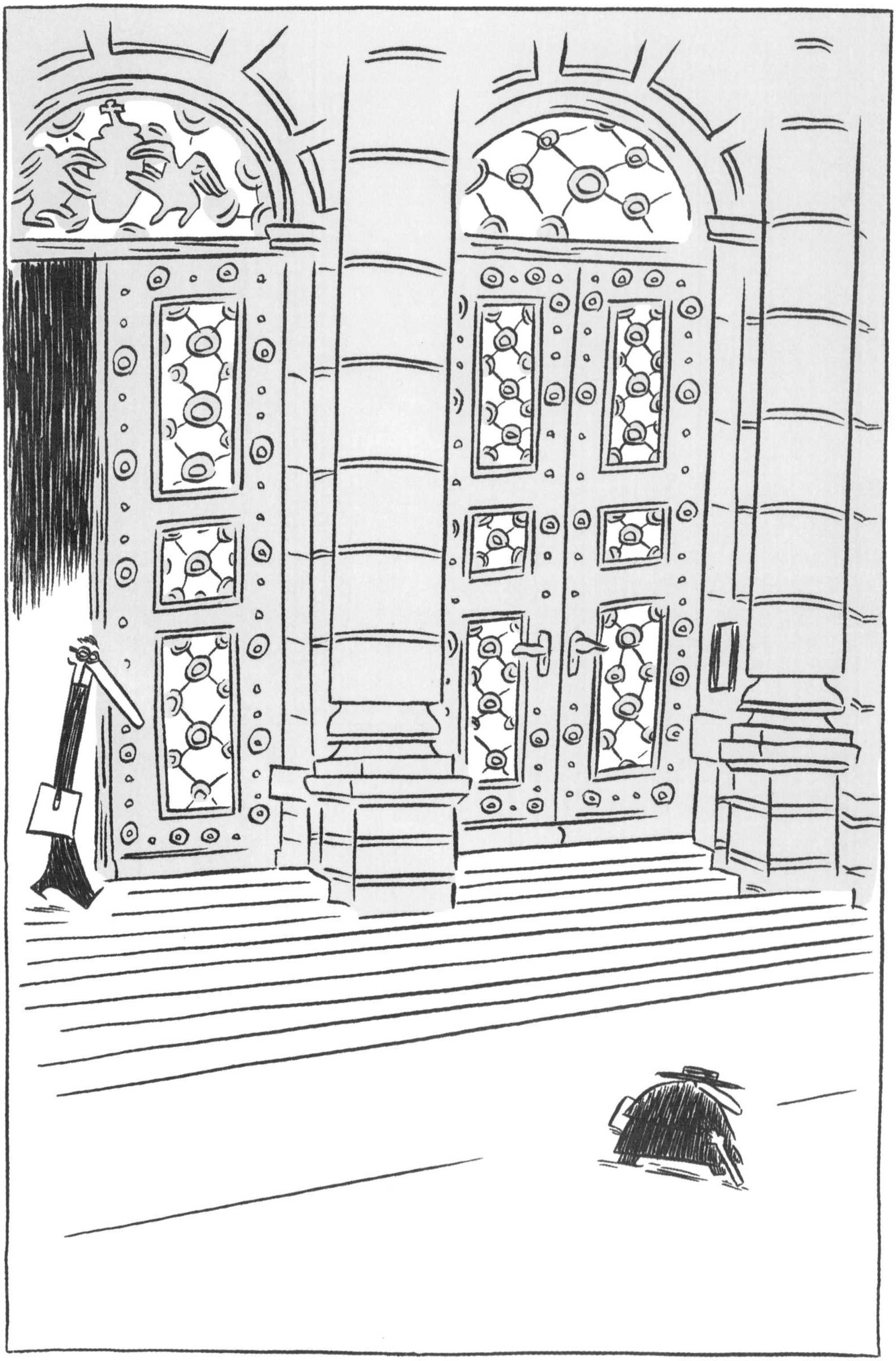

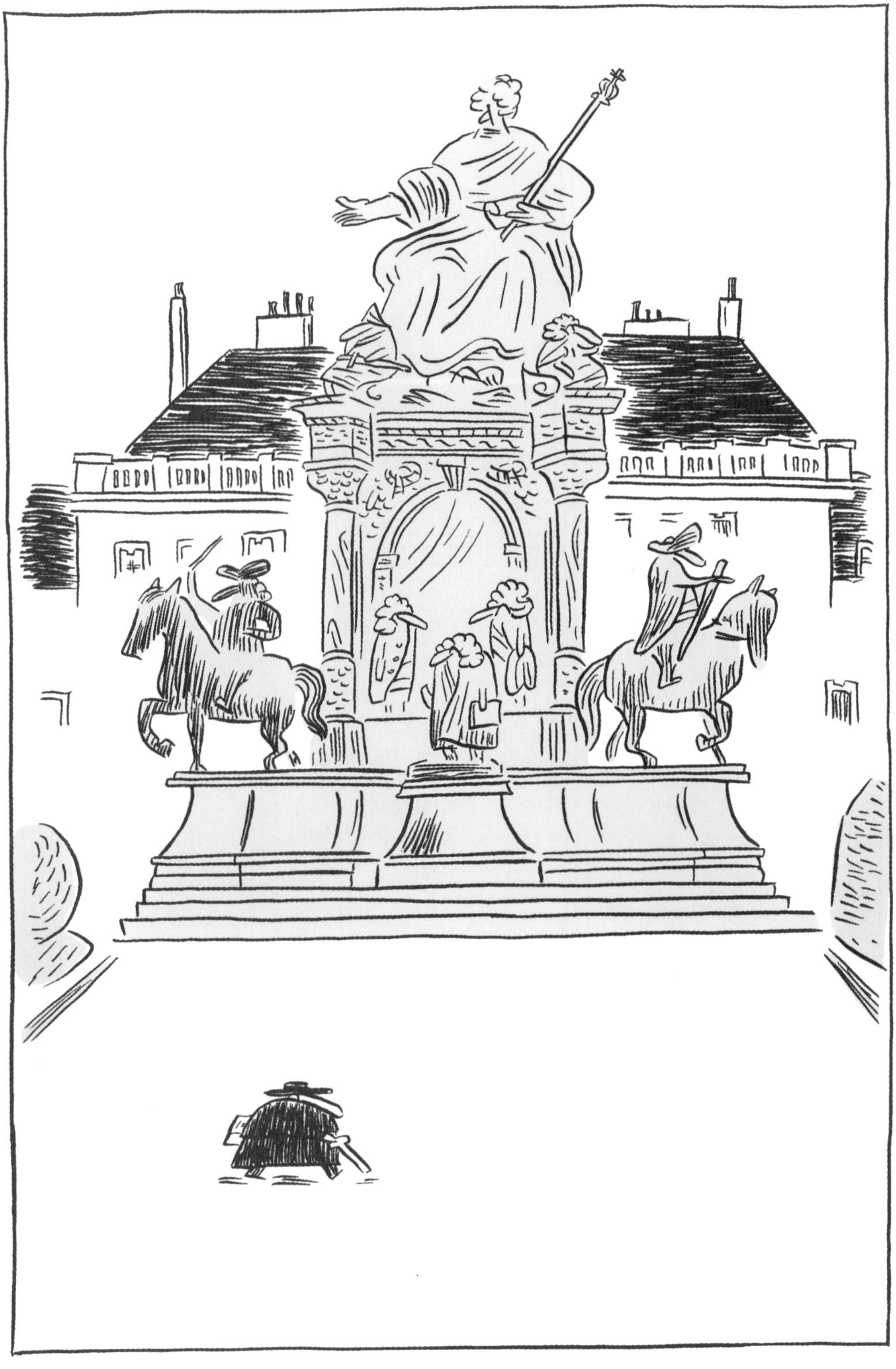

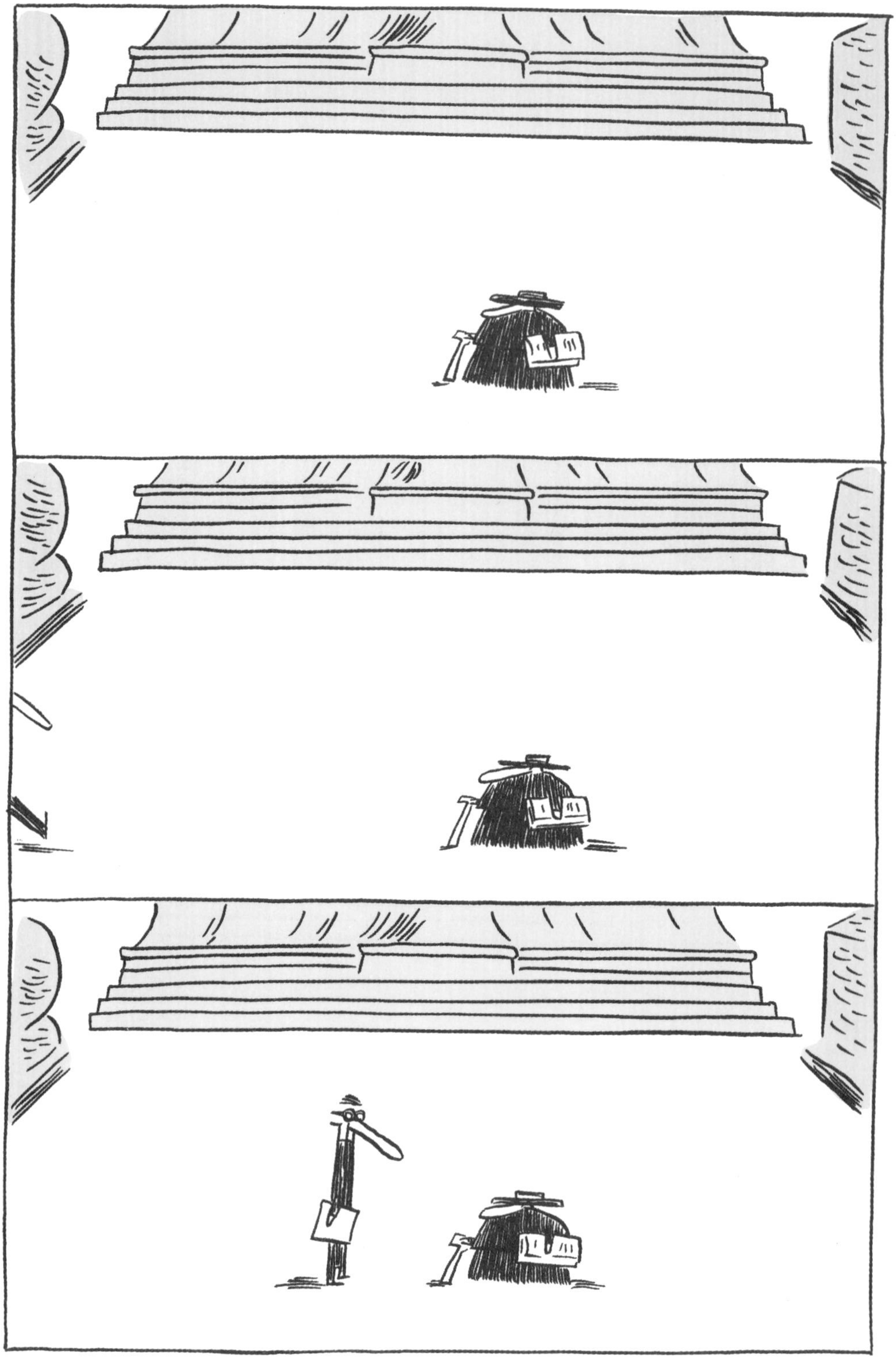

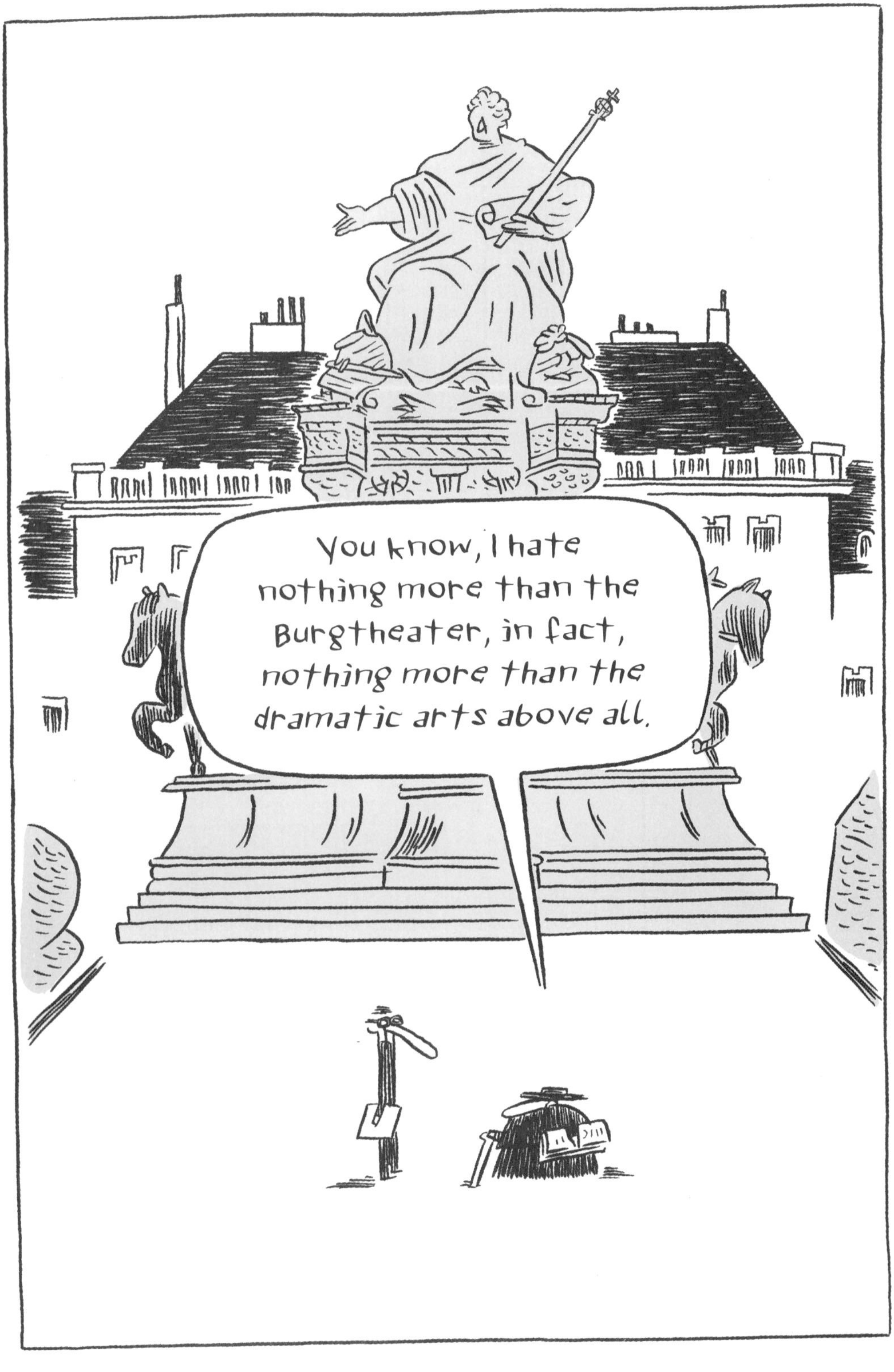
You know, I hate nothing more than the Burgtheater, in fact, nothing more than the dramatic arts above all.

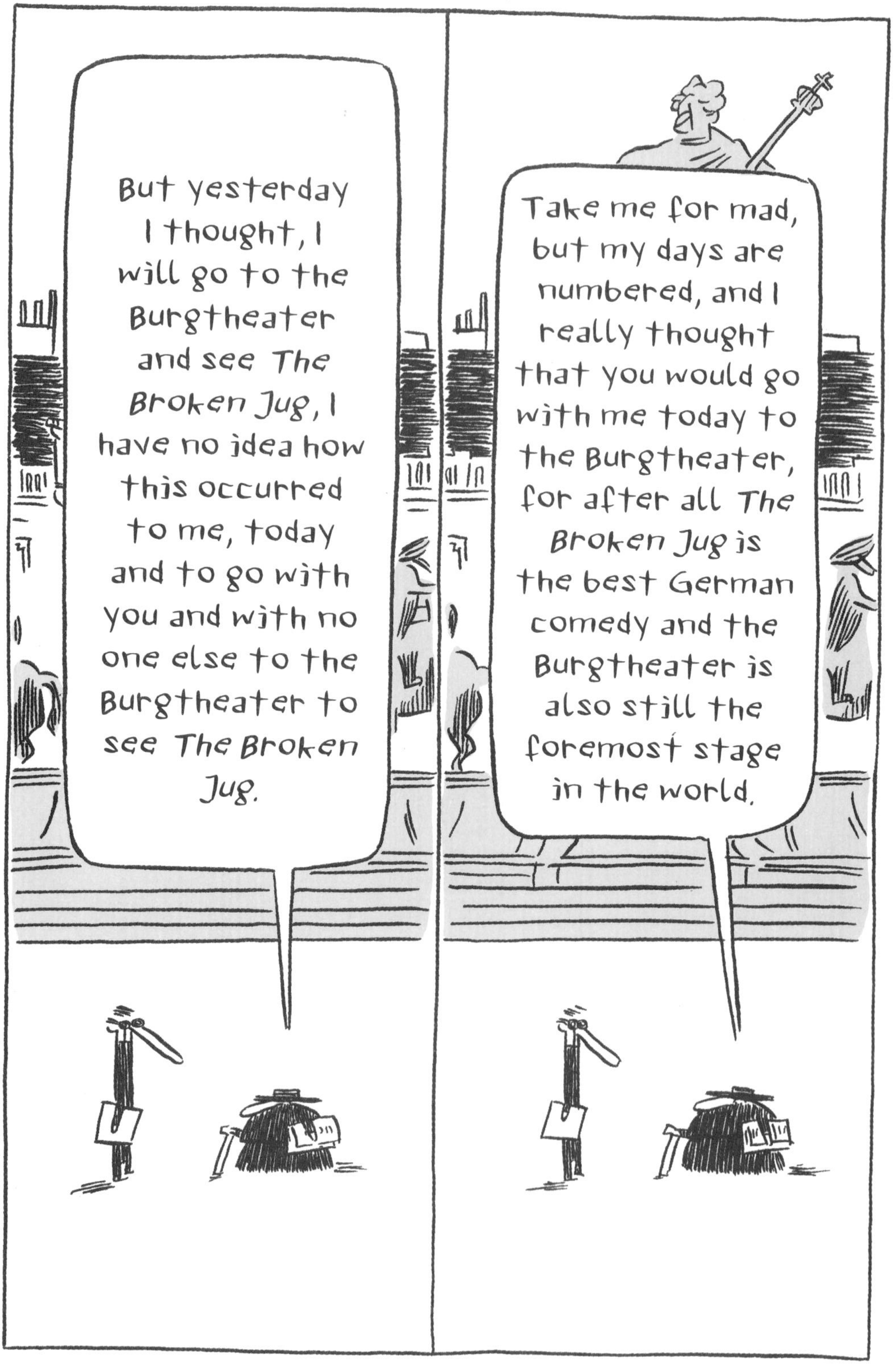
But yesterday I thought, I will go to the Burgtheater and see *The Broken Jug*, I have no idea how this occurred to me, today and to go with you and with no one else to the Burgtheater to see *The Broken Jug*.
Take me for mad, but my days are numbered, and I really thought that you would go with me today to the Burgtheater, for after all *The Broken Jug* is the best German comedy and the Burgtheater is also still the foremost stage in the world.

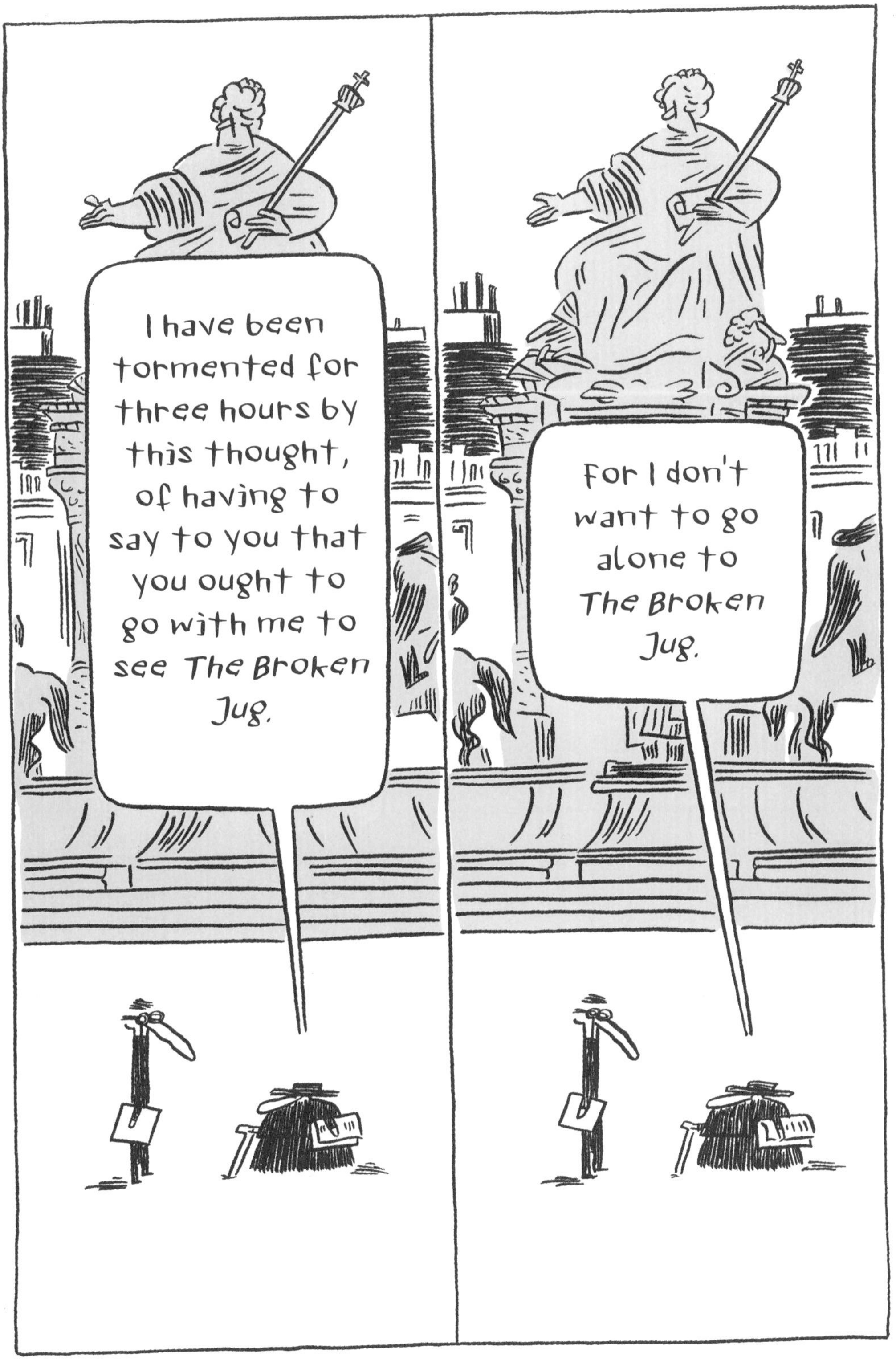
I have been tormented for three hours by this thought, of having to say to you that you ought to go with me to see The Broken Jug.
For I don't want to go alone to The Broken Jug.

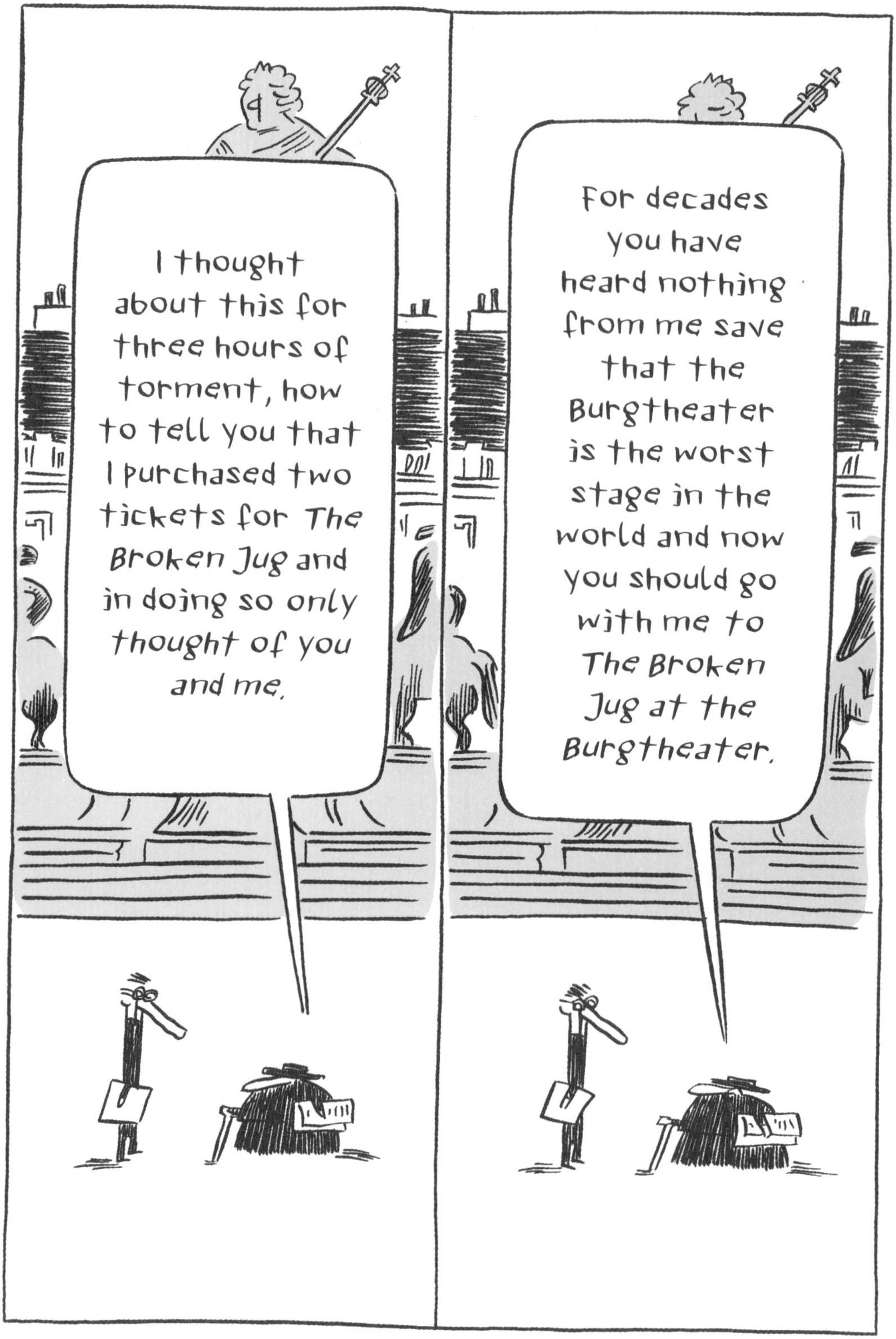
I thought about this for three hours of torment, how to tell you that I purchased two tickets for The Broken Jug and in doing so only thought of you and me.
For decades you have heard nothing from me save that the Burgtheater is the worst stage in the world and now you should go with me to The Broken Jug at the Burgtheater.

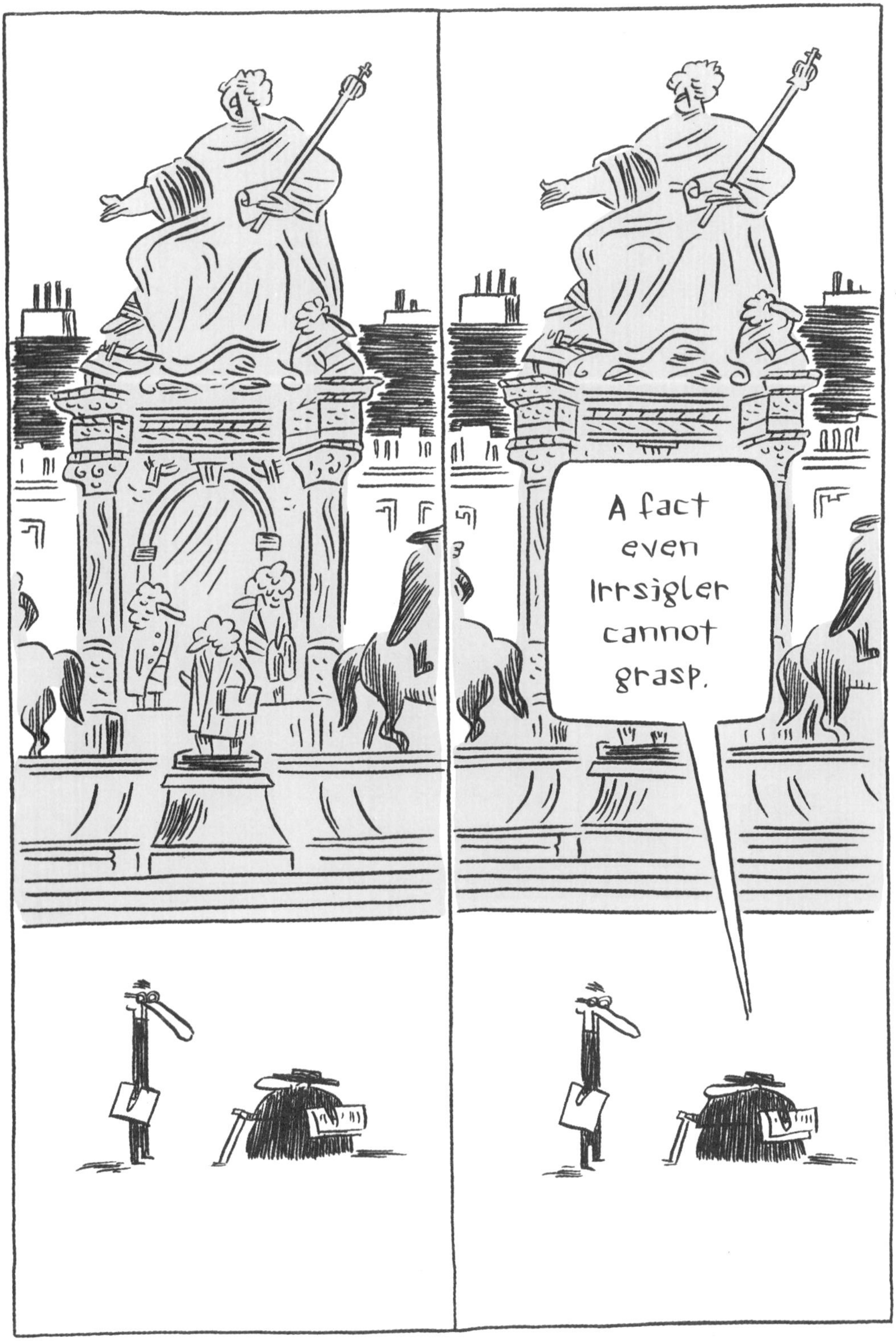
A fact even Irrsigler cannot grasp.

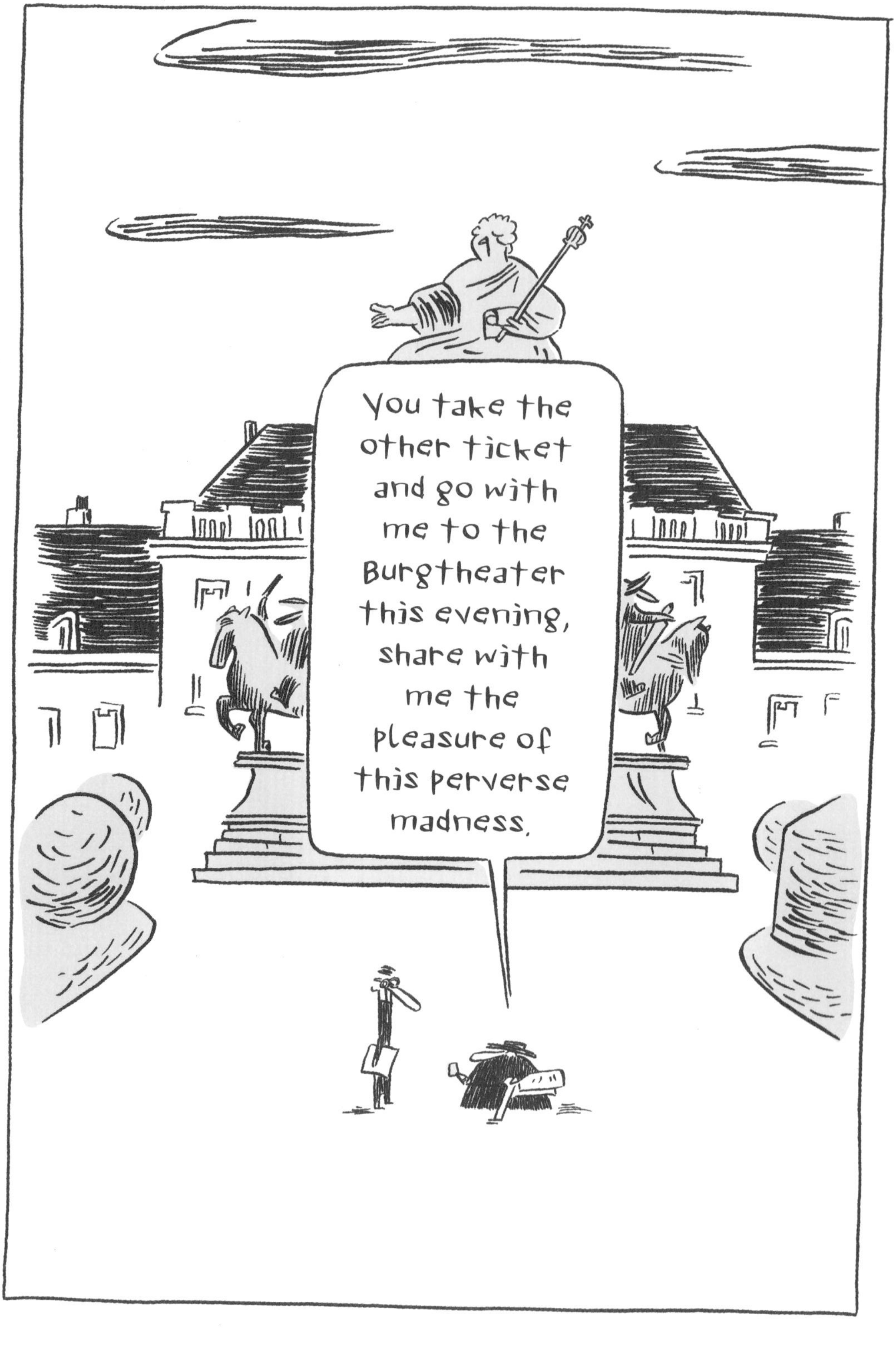
You take the other ticket and go with me to the Burgtheater this evening, share with me the pleasure of this perverse madness.

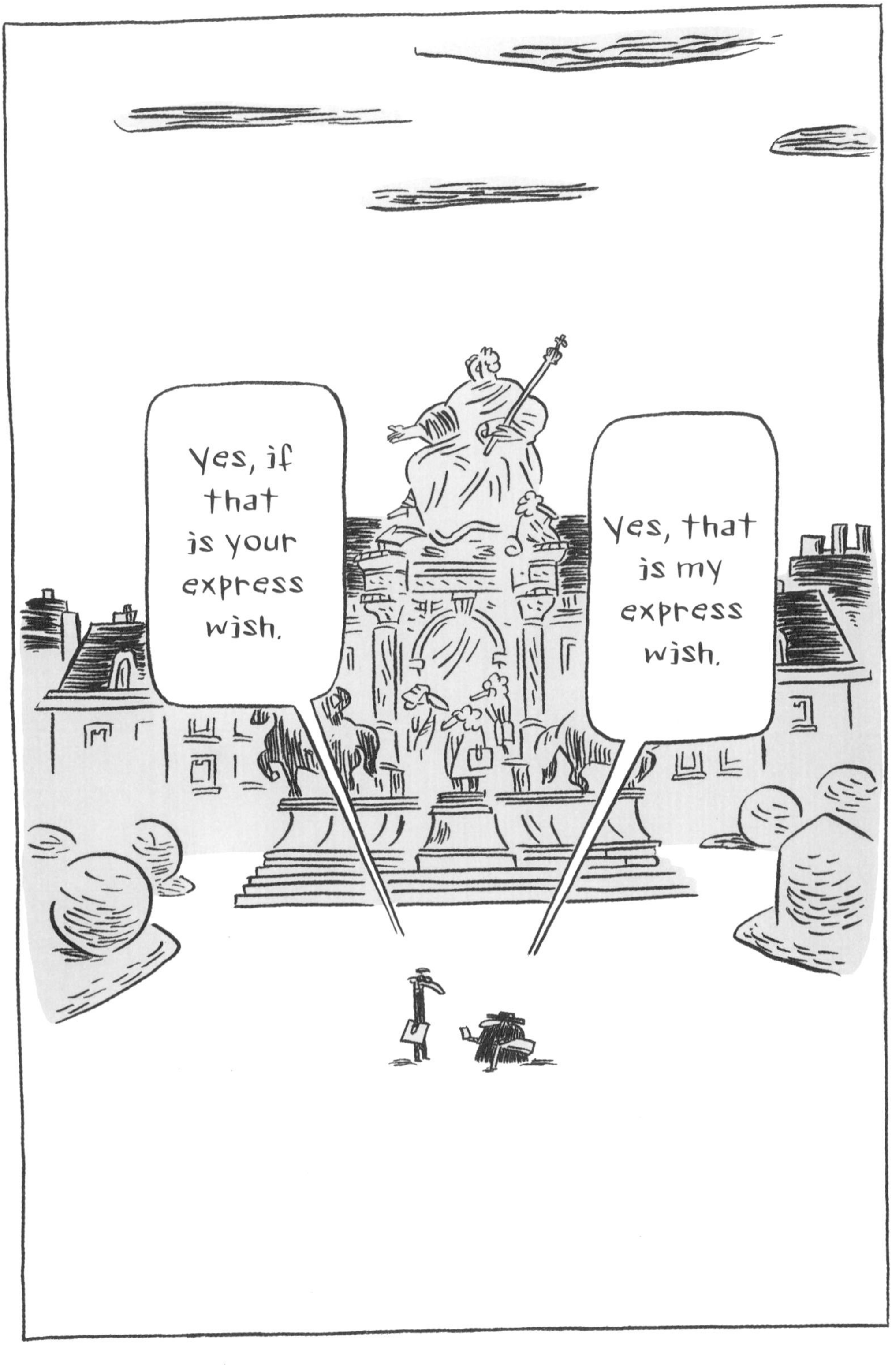
Yes, if that is your express wish.
Yes, that is my express wish.

That evening I really did go with Reger to the Burgtheater and to *The Broken Jug*.

The performance was terrible.